$12.95

Tinkerbell Jerusalem is a true story about how one person learns to appreciate whimsy and eternity all in one glimpse.

Through her discovery of a phenomenon she calls "inbetweens," **Bonnie Kelley Kaback** honed her ability to experience love and light.

Bonnie describes vividly how it feels to be a child surrounded by wonderful detail, but at the same time to be living in the midst of grown-up confusion. She takes bewilderment and gently breaks it down into bite-sized glimpses of truth.

Bonnie maintains she has always seen life this way.

The burden of watching her parents experience pain was often overwhelming— so she found a way to soften the picture. She looked at human unfoldment as a series of impressions, good and bad.

However, it was the glimpses of joy that brought her to a place where she could comprehend the lessons.

"Inbetweens are memories that have been transformed," Bonnie points out. "They're more evolved because they've been recognized and integrated on many levels of awareness. Linear time or events have no say in this matter. Inbetweens are eternal entities to be used as daily supplies."

This gentle approach to happiness is the perfect GIFT of love. Give it to yourself. Give it to a friend. And watch the magic unfold.

Tinkerbell
Jerusalem

Tinkerbell
Jerusalem

BONNIE KELLEY KABACK

Bonnie Kelley Kaback

THREE MONKEYS PUBLISHING

THREE MONKEYS PUBLISHING
1535 CROOKS RD.
ROCHESTER HILLS, MI 48309

Cover design by: Marc Myer, Laie, Hawai'i
Edited by: U'i Goldsberry
Photographs by: U'i Goldsberry

Manufactured in the United States of America

1 2 3 4 5 6 7 8 9 10

Library of Congress Catalog Card No. 96-60944

ISBN 1-889430-01-3 (H.Cover)
ISBN 1-889430-02-1 (P.Bound)

Lovingly dedicated to
my daughter Sara
and
my Granny Cravens

To Our Readers:

Why *Tinkerbell Jerusalem*? From the moment the manuscript came into our hands, we knew. There is an indescribable energy surrounding every project we are chosen to produce. Once again, a wonderful author has honored us with a gift and given us another opportunity to have fun doing what we love— publishing good books.

We believe *Tinkerbell* will strike an inner chord. Because it is a true story, there is assurance you can discover the "inbetweens" in your life. Take it from us, producing *Tinkerbell* was an inbetween, and will forever be a measure of quality and integrity for projects yet to come.

Thank you, Bonnie, you are Tinkerbell. And to the reader, thank you for buying this book. Pass it on with love.

with Love, Light, and Laughter,
Three Monkeys Publishing

On a personal note. . .

I have always felt that Divine Love is universal.
No one has a patent on it. If I have any religion,
it is simply to Love. My description of Jerusalem
as a city, represents my vision of Jerusalem as a
universal idea we all share. I honor it for this
reason.

Bonnie Kelley Kaback

ACKNOWLEDGMENTS

I would like to express deep gratitude to U'i Goldsberry, whose editing skills and insights helped shape this book. She worked with me every Friday morning for a year. She took my bits and pieces and wove them with her own tender "inbetweens."

I also thank U'i's husband, Steven Goldsberry, for doing the final edit of *Tinkerbell Jerusalem*. His suggestions from our first meeting were invaluable, and the ongoing respect he paid to my message gave me courage.

It was an honor to work with these two special people. They enhanced my life.

There are other individuals I wish I could thank for loving me in distinctive ways as I wrote this book. Each touch was encouragement. I try to share my appreciation as I go along in life, so I hope these cherished souls know how I feel.

To my publishers, Sally Cunningham Downey and Marilyn Schuster— I thank you for your readiness to expect good.

CONTENTS

BOOK ONE

Pixie Dust

"Will you make me some magic
with your own two hands?
Can you build an emerald city
with these grains of sand?"
Jim Steinman

Tinkerbell

     I reached middle age before I began to see as a child again. And what I saw were "inbetweens."

     The first time it happened and I understood consciously that a phenomenon had occurred, I was in the dentist's office, a place of heightened anxiety for a natural worrier. I hadn't thought about my father much lately. He'd died several years before. But I began flipping through a magazine, and I spotted a picture of a man fly fishing in shallow water on a sunny day. There was an unusual slant of light bathing the scene; it illuminated the red hunting jacket the fisherman wore. I was stunned. I had forgotten about Daddy's red plaid jacket. But at that moment the palpable memories of his old wonderful jacket came back to me: the softness of its wool, the musty hangs-outside-in-the-garage odor with the slightest hint of burning leaves, the way it went *swoosh-swoosh* when he gathered his little girl into his arms.

The rest of the day, including my dreaded hour in the dentist's chair, I thought of the good times I had as a kid with my dad, and the love and beauty of those moments filled me with bliss. I hardly noticed the drilling. The tedious errands I had to run that afternoon composed themselves into one seamless and easy expression, as though a symphony accompanied my every move.

For many reasons life seemed chaotic in those days. But here in the midst of appointments I thought would be horrible there came an image of a sunlit red jacket, and everything transformed.

It would not stay transformed. Like everyone, I had problems that pulled me back into dark moods. But then, in between the darknesses, I would notice other bright images showing themselves: a constellation of streetlights through a rainy windshield, the sound of bamboo wind chimes, a ballet recital for five year olds. And as these "inbetweens," as I came to call them, began flaring more and more often, the power of their light changed my outlook on life.

I said I saw as a child. When we grow up we become logical and pragmatic in ways that blind us to certain brightnesses. Good photographers tell us they have an eye for light. They don't focus on an object; they are attracted by the light playing over the object. I believe children have an eye for spiritual light, something metaphysical that makes an object or person glow with an energy that edifies because it penetrates deep into the soul. Inbetweens are carriers of this spiritual light. And it takes a childlike quality to see it.

Anything can be an inbetween. Any person at a particular moment can be an inbetween.

What inbetweens provide goes beyond mere delight. They lift us into a new dimension of acceptance and peace and harmony. Of love and beauty.

The magic of inbetweens reminded me of Tinkerbell. She waved her wand, and pixie dust cascaded like glitter over the Darling children. They floated up out of the mundane and flew with Peter Pan. Their flight was a new perspective, a metaphor for the power of the human mind.

Once I understood what inbetweens were, I saw them everywhere. Not only in my present, but in my past. I began collecting them, and taking notes on their meaning to me.

Without knowing it I had embarked upon an investigation that led me to an even more startling discovery. I kept thinking inbetweens were just a little pixie magic, occasional glimmerings come to rescue us from our muddled lives. In fact, they were clues, markings on a treasure map I didn't even know I was following until I found the treasure.

And then I would see— as a grown-up child— something so remarkable in its simplicity and wonder, it would change my life forever.

Magic Everywhere

Before that one terrible year that darkened the life of our family, I had a childhood without inbetweens. There was no need for them. Everything was bright and shimmering and new.

My earliest memories of joy are of Christmas time. I was the oldest of three children, so I had the honor of helping Daddy select our tree. I went with him to the tree farm, picked out a big bushy fir, cut it down, and with some help tied it to the roof of our car.

When we got home, I ran like a town crier through the house. "Mom! Mom! We got the absolute best tree on the lot!" I detailed to my little sister and brother the selection and the cutting and the adventure of getting the Christmas tree home.

Mom and I went to the attic and got the ornaments while Daddy trimmed the trunk in the garage then brought the tree into the living room. He fixed the green wonder to its stand and when he stood it up the tree filled the room with pine scent and the electric anticipation of Santa Claus and all the presents to come. I carried in the small boxes of ornaments and set them down like dusty offerings before the magnificent tree.

We spent hours shining familiar baubles and testing the lights. Daddy got on a ladder and wove the shining colors through the boughs. Then, while Mom kept reminding us, "Be gentle with that one, be gentle, they're glass," we hung the ornaments.

Silver and gold bulbs and hand-painted crystal birds rocked in the evergreen. Daddy pointed out each of the birds to his little kids. "This is a cardinal," he said. "This one's a robin, here's an oriole." And we mouthed the names of summer birds on our winter tree. Their feathers, streaked with brilliant blues, reds, and yellows, made them look like they were darting through the branches, their shiny foil tails stiff and sparkling.

My favorite spot was under the tree, lying with my head between the presents, my legs splayed out from under a pink flannel nightgown, my feet wiggling in little white wool socks. I blurred my eyes, turned the multicolored lights into stars, and watched their reflections on the round metallic-colored balls.

My mother said, "Bonnie's under the tree again."

And my dad laughed. "She's fine."

"She thinks she's a present."

"She is," my dad said. "Let's tie a bow to her feet."

I stayed there for hours, dreaming of a fantasy land where every day was Christmas, every breeze smelled like pine, and everything was coated in sugar.

When the holiday ended, one of my friends said, "I hate my house the day after Christmas. The magic is gone and it's so empty."

I didn't understand. That was my favorite time. There was more room under the tree for me.

When the day came to take the decorations down, I helped pack the precious ornaments into their boxes, each one snuggling into its own cardboard compartment. Then Mom and I carried them up to the attic. I followed Daddy into the yard when he took out the tree, and I kept going back to it so I could smell the fading piney perfume.

But the magic never ended. I still close my eyes and remember the twinkling.

Lace Trimmings

It was the morning of the first day of third grade. Mom called through the hall doorway, "Hurry up, Bonnie. Pick out something nice to wear and come down for breakfast."

Butterflies tickled in my tummy. "Will I make friends in my new class? Will the teacher like me?"

I put on my underclothes and some socks. The polished, wooden floor in my walk-in closet was slippery. I got distracted and slid around for a while in my stockinged feet.

I loved that.

My clothes hung on a convenient pole where I could easily reach them. "This rod is perfect for my height," I thought. "Someone planned this closet just for me." I felt so independent.

I noticed my blouses. There were so many favorites, I saved that choice for last. I picked out a grey flannel skirt with pleats, put it on, then glanced again at the blouses. I adored them. The row of lightly starched, crisp white cotton sleeves looked like proud soldiers in single file.

But there was something new about them!

My mother had added lace trim to every one. Cotton crocheted roses, snowflake designs, and delicate eyelet peeked out from under collars. They were beautiful. On a shirt's breast pocket I recognized the pattern of an old lace hankie my grandmother kept in her top dresser drawer.

I pulled the blouses out one at a time to examine them closer. I realized that Mom loved white blouses as much as I did. Delighting in the discovery, and completely forgetting my nervousness about school, I made my selection, then raced downstairs to thank her.

"Mom, you sewed lace on my blouses. They are just like brand new!"

She stood by the stove. We were alone in the kitchen. "Turn around and let me look," she said.

I spun and giggled.

"Wonderful," she said, smiling. "See how a tiny change can make a big difference?"

The Attic

Then a big change happened, the bad one.

I was nine years old the morning the grown-ups came to our house. Neighbors, friends, and relatives talked in hushed voices, sat on chairs, and created a heaviness that filled every room with sadness and confusion.

"He was driving the new Olds convertible," a neighbor said. "He ran smack into that oak tree at the fork in the road. Didn't even put on the brakes. It's a miracle he's alive the way the car looks."

I remember Mom's agonizing exhale. "But there's a good chance he'll pull through."

"Of course," someone said. "A good chance."

Daddy was hurt.

I ran upstairs. The small white door in the corner of my bedroom led to the attic. A shiny gold knob made it look like the White Rabbit's door in *Alice in Wonderland*. My mom and dad had to bend over to get through it and duck all the way up the narrow staircase, but I could walk right in.

The attic was my secret sanctuary, a place where I could stretch out my arms and fly to the land of daydreams. That morning I wanted only to be alone, to climb as high away from the voices as I could.

The attic's tall, pointed roof looked like a capital A. Thick, very puffy silvery material, tucked tightly in the crevices, covered the ceiling. It billowed like soft, floating clouds on a summer day, and shimmered with sprinkled stardust, like heaven.

Boxes along the walls spilled wonderful things all over the floor. Christmas ribbons, old worn-out shoes, silk scarves, a fur piece shaped like a fox, a big wide-brimmed hat, and my baby toys invited me to play.

I ran to the box where I kept my favorite stuff. I pulled out Daddy's old wool hunting hat and Mom's black suede pumps and put them on. Then I reached back in, and under an assortment of stuffed animals I found the music box Daddy brought home from a trip to Chicago.

It was a glass globe on a wooden pedestal, filled with water and tiny pieces of silver and gold glitter. Perched in the center, in a field of pastel flowers, danced a delicate fairy. She balanced in an arabesque, her bluish-white gown flowing in frozen movement. A tiny white dove nestled in the palm of her left hand. In her right she held a wand with a gold star, poised to bless the little dove.

Balancing in my mother's heels, I walked to the small plate-glass window in the center of the gable wall. I sat in the filtered sunlight and turned the music box key. It played "Für Elise." I held the globe up to the light and shook it and watched the sparkles tumble.

While the adults weighed each other down with their somber voices, I was pirouetting in my imagination, twirling with my glass-globed fairy in the pixie dust. We danced and danced together like sisters, soaring in fantasy and magic.

I didn't know it then, but this was the first time I sought out an inbetween.

Pinch Me

"Pinch me so I won't fall asleep."

These seven words kept me from feeling free for almost forty years. My father said them late one night as I huddled close to him in the car. This was before the accident, and before the other accidental mayhem that began occurring in my life.

Daddy was a country doctor. He took me with him on house calls. If he woke me in the middle of the night it meant there was a special patient who really needed him. I got to carry his black medical bag, sit in a cozy kitchen, eat cookies, and drink hot chocolate.

Everyone loved Daddy. When he smiled, his eyes twinkled and sick people felt better.

This particular night I felt an urgent seriousness about my job. When he bent over and said, "Pinch me so I won't fall asleep," his tone was soft, but very firm. It sounded like an order, not a request.

His eyes battled to stay open as we drove.

I found out years later that Daddy was addicted to morphine. He developed kidney stones as a teenager, and the drug controlled the pain. After he became a physician he started using it again. The morphine made him drowsy.

That night I became an official good citizen.

Our car lights lit a row of trees that lined the side of the road. I could barely see over the dashboard. The muffled hum of the engine made me sleepy.

"Daddy is driving a car in the middle of the night," I thought. "It's my mission to watch over him." So I pinched myself to stay awake, and I talked to him, to his eyes really, to keep them from drifting.

When I look through our old family photos I see a smudge-faced, sometimes dreamy, very giggly little girl. After age eight Mary Poppins took over. Everywhere in the albums there are snapshots of a posed, prim and proper young lady with a protective arm thrown around my brother or sister.

I thought a lot about being capable in those days. The carefree little girl changed into a cautious caretaker. I clutched my new position of honor. I thought no one would survive without my help.

Daddy's morphine led to the accident that almost killed him. I retreated to the attic when I first heard the news, but later I felt guilty because I wasn't with him in the car. It happened during the day, and I only rode with Daddy on those special house-call nights. But my sense of responsibility extended beyond any reasonable limit. My father had fallen asleep at the wheel. It had been my job to prevent that very thing from happening.

His crash caused serious head injuries. Daddy lay in a coma for weeks, and after regaining consciousness he suffered seizures. I remember the day the three of us went to the hospital to see him. His bed had metal bars on it. A big bandage covered his hair and ears. His legs and arms extended in four directions, attached to ropes. I saw pity in the eyes of the nurses as we approached his bed for the first time.

My mother explained about the bars. "Sometimes Daddy shakes all over and this way he won't fall out of bed," she told us. He opened his eyes and looked at his family without the slightest bit of recognition. I forced myself to turn away from those blank, distant eyes. Mom said to me, "Bonnie, why don't you take the kids for a little walk in the garden?"

She came out later and sat us down and said, "Daddy has amnesia. This means he can't remember certain things."

"Like what?" I asked.

"Well, he does remember that he's a doctor."

"Does he remember the accident?"

"No," she said.

"Does he remember us?"

She took a breath and straightened her back. "No," she said.

He couldn't remember anyone, in fact, except his nurse, who'd been in private practice with him for a few years before the accident. She had become a family friend.

When the seizures subsided he moved back to our house. What fanfare when he arrived. A whole crew of medical people came along to install him in the bedroom. My parents had French doors opening onto the yard and lake, so it was decided his rehabilitation should begin at home.

Daddy couldn't walk. It took months before he could stand without lots of help. In the meantime the family tried to rebuild our relationship with him artificially. We told him stories about each other, trying to make it as much fun as possible. He would nod and smile. He was a good man and he wanted us to believe he remembered a few things. But he was pretending, and I think even my baby sister could tell.

A year after the accident he was strong enough to work and see patients in his den next to the living room. One day while my mother was out grocery shopping, I was in the kitchen doing homework. The telephone rang. I picked up the wall phone at the same time he picked up the line in the den. I overheard an urgent conversation. "I love you and only you," he said. "I am going to leave her."

I felt it was my duty to inform my mother. I remember she came home with a bag of groceries and started putting them away, and I said, "I heard Daddy say something on the phone."

She started to look up, but then turned her eyes back into the bag. "What?" she asked.

From that day through the rest of my father's life, I suffered an emotional amnesia. I forgot the man who had raised me so tenderly for my first nine years, and I saw only this other partial Daddy. I blamed myself for the car accident. And when he left us and married his nurse, I blamed myself for telling my mother what I heard him say on the phone, as if that played a part in his decision. But that's how I was: so very responsible, so filled with baseless guilt.

It wasn't until that day in the dentist's office, four decades later— when a red hunting jacket shone from the page of a magazine— that I began to rouse myself and remember what I held dear about my father.

All those wonderful autumns before the accident, he wore the red jacket when we raked up the oak leaves in the front yard. He would prepare careless piles and let me run and dive into them. The big, final pile I could jump into only once. Then he made me stand at a safe distance while he lit the fire. We watched orange flames rise up from the orange leaves, making cloud-white billows that climbed the still air as high as I could see.

In summer we went out on the lake by the house. Daddy practiced swan dives and jack knives from the twelve-foot board he built at the edge of the dock. He said, "Dive for me, Bonnie. You dive better than anyone I know." He tread water under the board and assured me. "Just jump. I'll catch you." I plugged my nose, closed my eyes, and threw myself with little-girl clumsiness into the void. "See what a good diver you are?"

Daddy gave me detailed instruction about fishing and he never once hoarded a worm. I listened to endless facts on the crucial distinctions between a garter snake and a poisonous one. We played horseshoes out back on the manicured lawn, right next to the edge of a murky marsh. "Don't ever go into the marsh, "Daddy said. "There are big grey rats living in there."

He taught me to climb trees. Being in the branches was far more fun than playing with dolls.

He loved opera and cried when he described *Madame Butterfly*.

He cooed to his patients, whether they be adults or children, or wounded birds, raccoons, or dogs. He treated them all with gentle care.

He assured me that breathlessness was fine when you love something, and that glee was not the least bit silly.

I remember kisses on the forehead at bedtime, hugs, ice cream cones on hot days, little tickles under my chin, and piggyback rides. My father's love still glows strong in my heart.

Seven little words, "Pinch me so I won't fall asleep," changed the way I approached my life. Since that night I had assumed responsibility for everyone I loved. If they experienced failure, it was my failure, or my duty to fix it.

It wasn't until the red jacket that I realized the simple purity of love, my father's love for me and my love for him.

Beyond the darkness of the morphine and the accident and spiraling confusion of later years, the good memories endure. The jacket lifted me to a higher consciousness and allowed me to heal the pain associated with my father. In a way it pinched me out of my sleep of forgetfulness. I could reclaim my father. And in so doing, reclaim myself.

I recognize the worth of my father's gifts now, and my worthiness to feel his tickle.

A Crack in the Statue

My mother I have yet to reclaim. But I began the process recently by creating an inbetween for her.

Growing up, I thought Mom was a perfect person. In my imagination I molded her into a Grecian goddess set securely on a marble pedestal in a garden of pink flowers. She loved geraniums. Pink was her favorite color, although she insisted on red geraniums for the wooden window planters fronting our house. She pointed out knowledgeably, "Red sets off the grey bricks better."

Mom designed our house. She called it "The Dream House."

She dreamed a lot when she was young. She filled her photo albums with pages of extravagant poems glued tightly next to an array of pictures of her and my father. I remember one shot of Daddy wearing striped Bermuda bathing trunks and lounging on huge boulders alongside Lake Huron in Michigan. And another of Mom smiling resplendently with dark red lips. She modeled a slinky silk dress, wrinkled just the right amount, and wore a huge wide-brimmed hat and matching scarf.

She saved old invitations to social events, descriptions of lively festivities, newspaper clippings of her engagement to Daddy, and announcements of other young couples' betrothals.

Painstakingly positioned in the center of an arrangement of pressed flowers was a dog-eared magazine clipping titled, *The Woman in Love*. It described my mother's attitude perfectly. She grew up around the corner from my dad and it's rumored she loved him since kindergarten. She believed in the divine decree that "love is monogamous." Never for a moment did she imagine the possibility that commitment would not pan out for her.

Today my mother would be described as a woman who "loved too much." According to what I can deduce from the photo albums, her motives were simple and romantic. She expected joy and charm to be natural attachments to marriage.

One of my earliest memories was jubilation. I was three years old, playing in a bathtub of bobbing bubbles and toys. Mom walked in briskly, elated. Joy radiated everywhere. I think joy was the first emotion I consciously acknowledged.

She said something about Daddy. World War II had taken a number of men from our town. She said something like, "Daddy is a doctor. He doesn't have to go to war. He gets to stay home." I wasn't sure what her words meant, but love leaped out and grazed my heart.

Whenever I got sick she served me breakfast in bed. She would prop pillows up for my back and place a turquoise aluminum tray on my lap. My favorite meal was a poached egg on toast, cut in quarters, with slowly melting lumps of butter from the ice box, and small tumblers of freshly-squeezed orange juice and very cold milk. My mother's delicate doting made it fun to be sick.

Everything in "The Dream House" resonated with her sense of order. Even our linen closet opened upon a scene of peaceful charm. The sheets lay pressed and folded and organized into thick, straight columns.

The fluffy, sweet-smelling towels were grouped according to color and type. Bath towels, hand towels, and washcloths she had arranged in sets.

I felt the harmony of careful neatness when I looked into Mom's linen closet. It reflected dignity and grace, so I assumed she felt peaceful too. Her face completely masked anything unpleasant. Human perfection was something willed into existence.

I carved my own emotional demonstrations using her chiseled facade.

I am a lady today because of my mother. She instilled in me a sense of grace and style. I acquired impeccable direction by following each intricate nuance she presented. She stood erect and strongly balanced.

Shortly after my father's accident a crack formed in the statue. I'm not sure exactly when it happened, but my Grecian goddess ultimately shattered. Maybe it was Daddy's morphine addiction, or the automobile accident, or the amnesia. Or his leaving. Or maybe they all combined into a forced admission that a woman in love doesn't necessarily retain lifelong rights to her man.

There was something else too. After Daddy married his nurse he did not leave our lives. They had an apartment close enough that he could visit us often, and it was very strange. He lived happily for twenty-five years with another woman. Maybe the sight of his contentment without my mother is what broke her apart.

Whatever the reason, she became an alcoholic.

I never saw her cry before she turned to drinking. Disorder projected itself quickly. No more breakfasts in bed on sick days. In fact, very soon, breakfasts were sporadic. The linen closet opened to crooked, mixed-colored stacks of hastily folded cloth.

It nearly killed her, but after thirty years with the bottle, she finally quit. By then I was grown up and had moved away. I'm not sure what gave her the strength to dry out. Maybe Daddy's death helped.

These days my mother lives in a nursing home. She has little memory left. I visit a couple times a week, but it's been hard communicating with her. I say something. She says nothing. I say something else, and she says, "Stop trying to cheer me up."

One day after I discovered the power of inbetweens, I decided to create a special one for her. She sleeps late, and my plan was to serve her breakfast in bed on a turquoise tray.

It was very difficult finding a tray that approximated the ones we had at home. It took days of shopping before I finally located a matching set of three in an antique shop. They were the wrong shape but the right color.

I walked through my front door with the turquoise bundle under my arm, and the phone was ringing. It was the nursing home.

"Your mother's had an accident," the director told me. "She fractured her ankle."

"I'll be there in an hour," I said. I put the aluminum trays into a shopping bag and took them with me.

When I arrived, a nurse directed me to the covered porch overlooking the garden. An afternoon shower had cleaned every blade of grass and flower petal to a shiny gloss. The shade of the trellised verandah hinted a soft green from the sunlight filtering through the leaves. Mom sat in a wheelchair near the railing, facing the splendid scene. She looked proud and regal, her back straight, and her fingers woven together, lightly resting on her lap. A crocheted afghan of pink and yellow roses covered her legs. There was a tightly-bound gauze bandage on her left foot.

My mother, my erstwhile goddess, my role model looked so pale. Her tiny frame seemed smaller than the last time I visited.

I put the bag of trays on the floor and pulled up a chair. "I was planning to visit you tomorrow morning," I said.

She glanced down at the bag then looked back into the garden.

"I brought you something," I said.

She shrugged. "I'm fine," she told me.

A nurse walked over and said, "We're having a special meal today. Would you like to join us?"

"Yes, I'd love to," I said.

For my mom's wing, all twenty-four residents, there was a birthday celebration honoring everyone ninety years or over. Each of the ninety-somethings received a pink or white carnation. Confetti covered the tables. Small balloons bounced around the floor. The staff served turkey, mashed potatoes, gravy, and cranberry sauce. A nurse explained the menu to me. "When you get old you should have Thanksgiving as often as possible."

An attendant appeared from the kitchen with a huge cake with the birthday names written in fluffy white, cloud-like frosting. Everyone got a good look before they cut it. Mom wasn't given a flower; she was only seventy-six. A man at her table teased her five times with the exact same words, "Where is your flower, Loreece? How come your name isn't on the cake?" She laughed the first three times and flashed here patient Midwestern smile. Then she ignored him.

"It's time for the entertainment," someone announced, and one of the most outlandish women I've ever seen strolled into the dining room. She wore an auburn beehive wig and a floral chiffon dress that bubbled and swayed as she walked. Large 1960-ish orange flower earrings dangled from short chains and swung with every step. She moved with the flair of a Latin dancer, and she slid onto the piano bench like she was getting behind the wheel of a Cadillac convertible. Her musical technique was as loud and flamboyant as her outfit. Displaying a well-cultivated Scott Joplin style, she plunged into "Oh, You Beautiful Doll," followed by "Pretty Baby" and other songs of that period. Her hands pounded the keys like a prancing pony.

The nurses and attendants lined the metal walkers next to the piano, and everyone moved in close to the music. Most of the residents needed to be turned manually. House-slippered feet tapped, hands clapped, heads nodded, and smiles made clouded eyes sparkle. The joint hopped with a wonderful display of passion and love of life.

Mom and I remained in our seats near the back window. This was so like her, to cocoon in self-imposed seclusion in a room full of gaiety. "Let's move up and join the party," I said.

She shook her head no, but the patient smile I saw earlier returned.

"You didn't get a piece of cake, Mom."

"It had too much frosting," she said.

Taking this as a culinary cue, I got up and went to the front desk, where I'd left the bag. I returned with a piece of cake on a turquoise tray, and I put it on the table in front of Mom.

She noticed it immediately. "Where did you get this tray?" she asked.

"I know it isn't exactly like the ones we had," I said. "I wanted to bring you breakfast in bed with it, but this will have to do."

She nodded. "You remember," she said. She picked up a fork and started eating the cake, frosting and all.

I felt like sobbing. But I didn't want to make this a big emotional scene, especially since Mom seemed unmoved. "You remember too," I said.

"Of course, dear."

"Look at Mrs. Fraser," I said. Mom's roommate, holding a cane, danced a geriatric version of the watusi. "She's having a great time."

Mom chewed her cake. She looked out the window.

"Do you remember how we danced in the living room in the house on Huppcross Road?" I asked. "I would stand on the beige sofa and jump up and down while you held my hands. Remember the songs we sang?"

She didn't respond.

"Remember the lullabies? I sang them to my daughter. She wouldn't go to sleep without a song."

Mom grinned. She said, "Did she have a favorite?"

"Yes," I said. "Hush, Little Baby." I sang the first lines.

"That was your favorite." She laughed. "Look at those people. You would think they never heard music before."

"They are having such fun, Mom. Let's move a little closer."

"I'm fine here." She patted my hand. "I like this song."

Our peppy pianist slammed into "You're a Grand Old Flag." An old veteran sitting next to us saluted.

"Can I keep the tray?" Mom asked.

"I brought you a whole set."

"Good," she said. "I can use them as gifts for my friends here. But I'll keep this one for myself."

At the end of my visit, I left Mom watching TV with a group of women. I kissed her cheek and said, "I'll see you in a few days."

"Bring me a sweater, will you, Bonnie?" she asked. "I want to spend some time in the garden."

Fairy Godmother

As I said, I would discover inbetweens were more than little beacons that prompted good feelings. In all, my journey toward understanding their true meaning would comprise five phases. Two I had already passed, the first of simply recognizing inbetweens, and the second of seeing that they could be created. The third and fourth phases began to unfold as I was still recalling inbetweens from my past, when I found myself becoming a new student for old lessons.

While I suffered through my growing years with a cracked statue and absent father, there was one person in our family who remained a guiding light. Granny Cravens. I called her my fairy godmother.

She and Grandpa owned a dry cleaning business on a very busy street in downtown Detroit. I grew up in the country, so visiting the city, the "motor city," was an adventure. The streets buzzed with cars. Brakes squealed constantly. Horns honked.

The little bell on the front door of Granny's shop jingled all day long, announcing the arrival of customers. I loved the activity and excitement. My senses danced to the rhythm of the shop.

Granny had tender cheeks that felt velvety to touch. Her brown eyes reflected love with every look. Smiles created all of the little wrinkle lines on her face. She talked about regular things, but the words flowed together like rays of sunshine. I never heard a sour note in her voice. In that enormous city, with thousands of strange sounds and people, I felt completely safe. She handled each situation with utter calm and grace and filled the shop with peace.

When I talked to Granny about Mom's drinking, she said, "Sometimes, it seems impossible to rearrange circumstances, but you can see more love in the picture by looking for tiny bits of good. Let patience have her perfect work."

I didn't understand everything she said, but the tone in her voice made me feel better. She had that effect on people. Everyone felt better around her.

A grumpy man charged into the store one day, throwing the door wide open and almost knocking the little doorbell off the wall. "The mustard spot on this suit hasn't been removed!" he shouted.

Granny stood behind the counter at the cash register.

He stomped over to her and threw the suit jacket down. Before he uttered another word Granny said, "Good morning, Mr. Wagner. How can I help you?"

He fumbled with the jacket, took hold of the corner with the spot, and shook it. "Look at this. I think you never touched it!" Sweat beads formed on his brow.

Granny lifted the jacket from his hand and said, "Just a moment." She turned and walked into the back room.

In a few minutes she came out and said, "I am so sorry, Mr. Wagner. Let us take this and see what we can do."

The man's posture relaxed.

Granny continued, "Would it be all right if you picked it up in a couple of days?"

She disarmed him. Her patience and demeanor put him at ease, and he nodded and smiled. "Thank you," he said softly, and he walked out of the shop, gently closing the door behind him.

Granny did real magic.

She radiated patience, humility, gentleness, forgiveness, charity, and joy, all at the same time and in every situation. It didn't matter how dense the confusion appeared, she never strayed from her thoughtful post. Like a precious gem, the beauty she reflected came from within.

The good she saw around her must have come from inside too because sometimes what I saw surrounding her didn't seem so good to me.

I learned to look through Granny's eyes. She perceived love everywhere and refused to give power to the dark side of human existence. She taught me that all thoughts are mirrored in faces, posture, relationships, daily activities, and then projected onto the screen of life.

"What we think, we become, " she always said. "Each of us is a pure reflection of our thoughts and attitudes."

Granny acknowledged love and let it envelop her entire being. She couldn't help but reflect it. She regulated the quality of her life by the quality of her thinking.

My real-life fairy godmother believed that each person can uncover the purest core from within. She never wavered from the position of reflecting goodness.

As I sort out the tidbits of my growing years with Granny, I'm able to reacquaint myself with her. And as I consider her attitude, her way of living, *she* becomes an inbetween. She had the ability to take the light of inbetweens and manifest it outwardly from her soul, so that everyone she spoke to, everything she touched, everything she did *glowed*.

Miss Paisley's Bugs

I think our best teachers intuitively work with inbetweens. Often their lessons continue to instruct us even after years have passed. Granny Cravens was such a teacher. Another was a real teacher in my high school. The kids called her The Dreaded Miss Paisley. Next to Granny, she left the strongest impression on my teenage years.

She wore sturdy rubber-soled Oxfords and loose-fitting flowered cotton dresses. Her dark brown hair sculpted her head with a perfect bowl-cut. Her blue eyes looked out from thick-lensed, horn-rimmed glasses. Her stern appearance matched the clinically Spartan nononsense classroom.

She scared me before I saw her. I perused, with panic, my class schedule printout for the fall semester of eleventh grade. All breath escaped me as I read the words, "Introduction to Biology, Room 46, Miss Paisley." Fear registered as a knot in my chest. Her reputation for being "the toughest teacher at Seaholm High" was a well-circulated truth.

On the first day of class, she hit us with her famous assignment. "I want you to collect," she said, lowering her glasses with practiced dignity, "fifty insects, and properly mat them. Your entire grade for the first marking period is at stake."

We had to successfully net, kill, spread, pin, and then research fifty squirmy creatures in order to label them to match Miss Paisley's high standard of excellence.

Absolutely unbelievable! Though I knew this would be the case, somehow I hoped Miss Paisley's long-standing position would have modified over the summer. No such luck. I became another delegate marching to her dictate.

There was an alternative, however. A friend of mine whispered a quick solution. "There's an entomology lab in Ann Arbor that sells all the insects," she said. "We could buy them and mat them. They come already tagged with the information we need for labeling."

Ah, the ingenuity of young minds. See a problem and solve it. We were confident of an easy "A."

This had inordinate appeal because collecting them "piece-meal" seemed like a total waste of time, given our new option. I would get them all at once, mat them, then move on to other things. This was a pleasant and practical idea. What difference would it make to Miss Paisley?

Bugs are bugs, for heaven's sake.

At the crack of dawn on a Saturday morning, we squeezed into my friend's car, on a mission of espionage. Only one of us had a license and that made the trip, with no parents, exhilarating. We had a blast!

At the insect lab we laughed and skipped playfully up and down the aisles making fun of the silly-looking bugs.

Matting them was easy. I turned in my completed assignment, fifty critters strategically pinned on colored construction paper glued to the bottom of cigar boxes. White, typed labels identified their classifications. Everything was correct, divided and color-coded, pinned, labeled, and submitted. I felt secretly secure about my creative finished piece.

We got our assortments back several days later. In glaring boldness across the top of my cigar boxes, now bound together with a rubber band, was a white sheet of paper with a big red F.

I'd failed! At what? I completed the assignment. All fifty bugs had been catalogued. The F stood out on the clean sheet, in full view, like a scarlet letter.

My friends received the same grade. I saw it in their faces.

In the right hand corner of the paper, in the neatest penmanship, Miss Paisley had written, "If you write me a note stating that you purchased the bugs and why, your grade will be raised to a C. No further discussion is necessary."

I prided myself in maintaining A's and B's. Getting a C meant disaster. I liked seeing my name listed on the honor roll, printed in the school newspaper. I liked being a good student.

"So I bought the damn bugs," I thought. "What's that got to do with anything? It's not even a truly academic assessment. How can she do this? Maybe she can't really tell. Maybe she's bluffing."

I wallowed in extreme self-pity and indignation for a while. Anger followed close behind. Then I dipped into the area of feeling ashamed, embarrassed. By the time I found myself on the bottom floor of the humiliation department, closed doors began opening. I thought about why she asked us to do this exercise. What could have been her motive? She surely didn't need more bugs for her collection.

Then I remembered what she said. "Collecting the bugs will be a painstaking process, and that is the importance of your work."

I had interpreted her words hastily and unjustly as exaggeration, as a teacher's proud hyperbole for some sort of grand effect she wanted to achieve. "Being tough is her intention, " I thought. "She wants to be difficult."

As a result, I didn't hear her message, or witness her gift. I plugged my ears and put blinders over my ability to see significance beyond the obvious. I totally missed her point.

What I thought was, "A bunch of bugs is the sole purpose of this plan," and I took a back road to reach the mark. I bypassed the miracles she hoped would be gathered along the way.

Of course, I told the truth and got the C. I didn't make the honor roll because what I'd done was less than honorable. I suffered for it internally.

I did some thinking about her message but the true weight hit home only within the last few years, after I had begun my exercise in understanding inbetweens.

What Miss Paisley wanted us to experience, as impressionable, peer-driven teenagers, was the wonder of discovery. She aimed to inspire us to see uniqueness in bugs, to spot them in their environment, to fly after butterflies and crawl with beetles.

My memories of Granny Cravens and Miss Paisley intertwined in ways I didn't expect.

In my exhilaration to learn an old lesson I might have missed, I decided I'd fulfill— finally, and to the letter— Miss Paisley's assignment. I went to the hardware store and bought a butterfly net. Then I stalked the yard for the first of my fifty specimens. Imagine a middle-aged woman trying to complete a childhood imperative. I felt really silly.

I want to make one thing clear about this process of acquainting myself with inbetweens.

Everything didn't happen chronologically. There were moments that clearly qualified as true turning points, but they were not like flashbulbs going off, like that bright hunting coat was. I wish my life were that easy. A couple of powerful experiences did result from my bug hunt, however.

I got an old mayonnaise jar and punched holes in the lid. This is where I housed my first catches. I swooped down on a thin, light-green grasshopper, rolled him out of the net, and placed him in the jar. He didn't jump around in there like I expected, but just stood in the center of the bottom, like a new leaf with legs.

Next I caught a monarch butterfly. It floated from under the bushy shadows into a sunray. The brightness of its wings, turning gold in the golden light, startled me. For a second I forgot my purpose. But then, with one pass of the net, I had it. I was gentle with the transfer to the jar. I didn't want to damage the delicate wings.

As I sat on the lawn, a lady bug presented herself on a blade of grass. I picked her up and dropped her in with the other two. And then I watched the bugs move around in their unhappy confinement.

How could I kill my tiny captives and pin them to a piece of cardboard? As a sensitive teenage girl how could I have done it? Can't I learn more about them if they're alive? I held the jar close.

The lady bug was a dot of red, gliding without legs that I could see, so it seemed a miniature hovercraft. And the mist-green grasshopper, animated now and leaping, and the fluttering orange monarch danced in desperation, bumping against the tight glass and tin lid. It was a soft, cool fire I was watching. My jar was a lantern burning with life.

I studied the insects for a long time, until they settled into a quivering stillness. Then I opened the jar and let them go. The lady bug disappeared in the grass. The grasshopper sprang into leaves almost its color, and blended away. But the butterfly took its liberty into a flight straight up, flapping its brilliant wings so high it sailed over the treetops.

I figured I'd again flunked Miss Paisley's assignment. The process of discovery was left incomplete. Still, for days afterward, what I'd witnessed collecting the bugs stayed with me.

Failure is usually opportunity in disguise. Maybe I had learned something after all.

I knew I created an inbetween for myself with my little exercise. But in this instance I had savored the moment. I let it soak in. Without realizing it, I had meditated on those luminous insects, and in so doing, I allowed the energy of their being to enter me. So what if I failed to carry out my original intention? I had succeeded at something grander.

This is when I hit upon the notion that inbetweens were carriers of spiritual light. Except that it wasn't just light in the sense I could see better; it was heat as well, or something akin to heat. It was energy. Positive energy. A subtle but irrepressible glory.

And *glory* is an energy source. The light surrounding those small creatures made a difference in me as the red coat had made a difference, except that now I had given the energy more time to connect. As the light was absorbed within me, it pushed into the doubts and negativity I had borne for so many years, the psychological pockets of darkness and cold. My personality, my attitude, my expectations, my everything became infused with this light.

And, more remarkably, I noticed that I could deliver the light to others.

Inbetweens were transforming me. Beyond being providers of momentary joy, they had the capacity, given time, to make me a more positive person. I felt the change take place slowly, and I kept in mind my Granny Cravens as the model for what I might become.

I wondered if I could recall inbetweens Granny may have used. Sure enough, as soon as I thought about it I remembered her household and especially the dry cleaning shop decorated with inbetweens.

In the apartment were the old framed photos, an heirloom jewelry box, a stuffed sailfish my grandfather caught, usual things that would prompt good feelings in any family. The shop downstairs held items with greater magic. Besides the small golden bell that announced customers opening the door, there were little hand-painted figurines; an angel on one side of the counter and a balloon lady on the other. The angel stretched out her arms as if to bless each bundle of laundry that passed by. The balloon lady sat on a park bench and clasped several wire "strings" leading up to balloons of bright yellow, white, and maroon. *Maroon balloons*, even the sound of the words is an inbetween. Granny also had tacked postcards to one wall, so while customers waited for their clean clothes they could gaze at Niagara Falls' plummeting waters, the Grand Tetons reflected in a lake, a pink sunset beyond the lighted Golden Gate Bridge.

But my favorites were the cut-glass prisms that hung in the shop window. The late afternoon sun would refract through the prisms, sending slices of rainbows around the white walls and paper-covered laundry. The rainbow bits drifted slowly, like the lost, intangible wings of fairies. If I tried to catch one, it leaped onto the back of my hand.

No wonder Granny seemed buoyed by a lightness of spirit. Even though she didn't call these things inbetweens, she clearly understood their powers. She had surrounded herself with objects that meant something to her, touchstones of love.

And she certainly created inbetweens for me. At least once a year she took me to the dentist's office. We rode downtown on the bus, and afterward we walked to Saunder's for lunch. For dessert, every time, she let me eat a hot fudge sundae. After having my teeth cleaned that sweet treat seemed incredibly delicious. And it was a little naughty; I felt like we had a secret. Usually, however, she found ways to make healthful food more appealing. She would add walnuts to her chicken salad, and she taught me to appreciate turnips by mashing them up for me.

Sometime during my memories of Granny Cravens and my attempts at bug collecting I entered the next two phases in my growing understanding.

First of all, I found that through meditation I could draw the light of inbetweens into myself. I don't mean meditation in the classic Eastern sense with breathing exercises, body positioning, and thought control. All I had to do was look at the object for a few moments, and the transfer of energy occurred.

As the light filled me I discovered something else. I was functioning as a source of positive energy for others. This is how my Granny operated, dispensing love in every situation, no matter how difficult. I had done this already with the turquoise trays. I would do it many more times in the months ahead. Interestingly, the more kindness I showed, the more kindly the world treated me. The more I helped, the more I received.

Now I have a confession to make. My initial discovery and subsequent study of inbetweens occurred during a period of accelerated crisis in my life. You should know, this is a sad and difficult story for me to tell. My seventeen-year marriage was ending in a very painful, protracted divorce. The hurricane of darkness that swirled around the break-up would have driven me crazy if it weren't for inbetweens.

BOOK TWO

Alchemy

"Let him that would move the world,
first move himself."

Socrates

A Sandwich of Substance

My luck with men hasn't been great. Psychologically I've lived in fear they would abandon me the way my father did, that they would forget the love.

It happened in my first marriage. Things came to an abrupt halt, and he was gone. There were good times before then. Rare good times, glimpses of hope. There was even what I think of now as the perfect example of an inbetween.

For a while we lived in London, in a small "bed sitter" flat in a narrow brownstone Victorian building. We were on the third floor just below the attic, where Martin Dickerson lived. I was quite impressed by Martin because he had graduated from Cambridge. He read "just for jolly good fun" novels I had labored over using Cliffnotes to augment my insights.

It cost a shilling to run the heater. We shared a bathroom with seven people, and the kitchen, two doors down the hall, had only a sink and hot plate, no fridge. Before we saved enough money to rent a small icebox, I stored our perishables outside on the window ledge. Our rent ran five pounds per week (about $10.00 American). The place was cramped, rather threadbare, and as grey as the weather.

We had one tiny closet, just large enough to hang a coat and dress. Everything was damp. One time my husband's trench coat molded to the wall. He peeled it off to wear it.

The Fieldings lived downstairs with their two delightful, round, and eternally rosy-cheeked children, in a regular-sized apartment with a living room (which they called the "drawing room," sounding terribly British). I loved our visits there. It felt so homey.

Renee Fielding gave her children marmite sandwiches at tea time. Marmite is a flimsy spread of meat extract smeared in a very thin layer between large slices of flat white bread. It amazed me something so simple could suffice as substance for a sandwich. However meager, the concentrated flavor satisfied the hungriest of palates.

Her children, James and Caroline, loved the sandwiches. The kids always ended up with brown smiles, marmite smudged all over their faces.

Now whenever I remember those brown, marmite-rimmed, smiling mouths, I think of inbetweens. They're like tiny glimmers of happiness, spread to faint impressions, sandwiched between large, thick slabs of mundane experience. Even if our filling is marmite thin, these sweet elements can create happiness and fill an entire day with joy.

Wandering Through a Maze of Rose Bushes

Life's lessons endure, in spite of how elementary they may seem at first. One emerged from the past recently, on the night of my friend Lauren's annual lavish Christmas party. She stood on the polished marble floor just inside the double oak doors and greeted her guests. As I entered the house, I noticed the wonderful smell of fresh flowers. At the foot of the staircase in the middle of the foyer she had placed a magnificent alabaster vase filled with a bouquet of two dozen white roses. Greenery and fanciful sprays of baby's breath surrounded each gentle blossom.

I said "Merry Christmas" to the family, then instinctively walked to the flowers. As I leaned over to smell the largest bud, Lauren whispered, "Be careful of the thorns."

The warning sounded odd, and out of place in all that splendor. I was experienced in handling roses and well versed in the danger of thorns. I hadn't thought of touching the flowers, but at that point I backed away to respect the potential for hidden pain. Almost as quickly, I am proud to say, I leaned over again and smelled the rose.

Thorns aren't so bad. They do surprise us when we touch them or bump up against them. They hurt, they sting, and sometimes they draw blood. Their purpose is to protect the roses, but they never distract from the radiance of the flowers.

I learned about thorns long ago, when my daughter was a baby, and as I stood admiring Lauren's bouquet I understood that my initial reaction to her warning was part of an old response pattern I was growing beyond.

My first marriage did produce my life's greatest gift, a daughter we named Sara, the Hebrew word meaning "princess." She was only a year old when her father and I divorced. So Sara and I ventured out into the world together.

We lived in Santa Monica, California. On a pier close to our apartment was a wonderful, run-down merry-go-round. Sara loved it. We went there once a week. Her favorite pony was white with a pink saddle, golden mane, and blue eyes. Each time I put her in the saddle she leaned forward and glided her fingers over the fluted surface of the mane, gently caressing the golden curls. I stood next to her holding her waist as the music began. We swung round and round. My little princess rode up and down with such joy in her sweet body. She giggled and bounced in the saddle, keeping time with the movement of the carrousel.

Some days I would watch her and think, "I'm alone with this child and I've got no one to share the experience." Sadness controlled these moments, and happiness cowered in the shadows. I wandered through an emotional maze, each corner identical to the others, every turn leading me in an endlessly stagnant pattern. Occasionally, I pricked myself with sharp intrusions of pain.

Thorns became my emphasis. I lost sight of the roses.

One day as I watched Sara's happy ride on her carrousel horse, an astonishingly simple thought came to me. "She's yours. You get to raise her." She was my precious gift and I had the opportunity to love her with all my heart.

That day we became the rosebush. We were together. My fear and loneliness faded, and I could embrace her beauty, her delicate core. No longer the victim, I gained purpose as her sole protector.

I think now that what I learned with Sara was to shift focus and concentrate on the blossoms of our relationship. Even though I'd spent half my childhood in a broken home, I was very traditional in my notions about child raising, and I couldn't imagine doing it alone. But I had no choice. Either I remained stuck in my thorny maze, to the detriment of both of us, or I changed my perspective.

You *can* change your perspective on the pain if you learn how to work around it, and concentrate on the beauty beyond.

As surely as there are thorns, there will always be roses.

The Gilded Cage

From the moment of her birth, Sara emitted a
light, a twinkling.

She cried and my heart wept. She moved and
my soul danced. She became my constant companion.
We shared everything. The decisions I made about my
job, recreation, relationships, food, all revolved around
her. I cherished our union and desperately lavished all
my affections on her little presence.

A part of me said, "This fresh quality you love
in Sara comes only from her. She holds a patent on it.
You can't exist without it. This is love."

At the age of two, Sara began to make
decisions. She selected outlandish outfits, a purple shirt

with blue plaid shorts, a yellow sundress on a cold grey day. She demanded my attention and exploded into tantrums of dramatic defiance. They call this expression of individuality the "terrible twos." Our lives lived up to the labeling. We were terrible.

Sara demanded and I complied. I provided her with everything I had in an effort to control her. We continued our off-balance relationship until she went to kindergarten.

Things changed. She settled down and her bright sparkle and effervescent love of life bloomed, filling every room she entered, everyone she touched, and every space in my heart.

I held her close, moment to moment, as if she were the air I breathed.

Both of us interpreted my response as love. I loved her totally, frenetically. Our lives continued, Sara making no demands because I supplied every anticipated need.

The modern term for this is "over-mothering." The old one is "smothering."

When she was five I remarried. But nothing changed my smothering attentiveness to my girl.

Adolescence is the second period of self-expression and exploration. My pattern was set, everything in order for Sara, everything perfect. The problem with this line of thinking is that my idea of perfection wasn't Sara's.

Her bedroom looked like a demolition site, laundry scattered everywhere. The television blared from the moment she entered her sanctuary of chaos, its din cluttering the air the way the clothes and books and papers cluttered the floor.

My friends suggested, "Close the door. It's her space. She's a teenager. She has to learn to organize herself. Besides, she's your daughter, not you. Her room should be off-limits."

How could I turn my back and walk away?

I didn't.

I cleaned and washed and organized everything. I made her bed, hung up her clothes, put away her school books, organized her drawers.

She used to say, "Mom, I can't find anything. It's too neat in here. I can't think this way. I need piles of clothes around. They make me feel cozy. I need the television on. I need the confusion."

Sara's insistence on messing up her room and the justification for her position slapped my hands. In her mild way she exposed my program of control and rebuked my domineering.

I wanted her to need me, to see me as an indispensable part of her life. The more I clung to her, the more she pushed me away. My fear of losing her propelled me into the need to control. I failed to see her independence as an expression of growth. I disguised my motives as love and began to stifle her.

This wasn't love. Love is not supposed to bring a sense of possessiveness, manipulation, jealousy, panic, or dysfunction. This was personal coveting, a clinging, fearful, restrictive, protective view.

I've experienced the deep pain provoked by the fear of "losing love." My craving for others mandated my existence. As long as I continued to anchor myself to another person, I was bound and beholden to that presence.

By fashioning an environment of control for Sara, I unwittingly invited the same situation into my life. As I projected my desperate need of her, I became the desperately needed.

This is one of the strange but observable realities of human existence. Some people call it karma. I don't know what to call it. But I've noticed in the patterns of where I go and what I do that there are reflections of my attitudes and state of mind coming back to me. When I forgive, I am forgiven; when I am angry, people are angry with me; when I seek to control, I am controlled. You've heard the time-honored maxims attesting to the phenomenon, things like "What goes around comes around." "Tit for tat." Another is "Do unto others as you would have them do unto you," because they will, or life will.

So, when I remarried I flowed right into the kind of predicament I'd forced upon Sara. My claustrophobic neediness projected back at me. My new marriage suffocated, trapped, and held me hostage in a beautiful home with cars and credit cards, a gilded cage that restricted all movement. My husband arranged everything. He took care of me like I was a favorite rare bird, with wings clipped and a tongue trimmed so I could speak his language.

He didn't do it maliciously. His actions were magnanimous, and laced with caring and humor. I think he felt a need to protect me. I've talked to and observed several of my friends, and such attempts at psychological shaping are a common practice, not only with domineering husbands but wives as well, although women tend more often to submit to male power.

My husband simply had in mind an ideal about the kind of mate I should be to complement his desires and ambitions, and he worked at molding me to fit that image.

To my regret and loss of personal identity, I acquiesced. How unlike Sara I behaved in this. She would rebel in little ways against my authority, at every turn. I, on the other hand, bowed my head and let it happen. Until I felt I'd lost myself and all my potential.

Then I exploded with one big rebellion.

I decided on divorce.

There's another story that comes into play here, speaking of control. When I graduated from high school, my mother gave me a ring. It had been given to her by Granny in ninth grade, for straight A's. Mom wore the ring for years. Its silver band eroded down to a thinness like bird bone. A tiny diamond chip nestled modestly in the raised setting. The ring had little real value, obviously. But for me there could be no finer piece of jewelry in the world. I wore it proudly until I feared the tenuous silver might break and I'd lose it.

I kept the ring wrapped in a handkerchief in a small flowered cardboard box. Once in a while I'd take it out and remember. Yes, it worked like an inbetween before I knew what inbetweens were. Then one morning it served as a real inbetween and more. It became a symbol.

I was rummaging in my dresser drawer for a pair of socks. I saw the small box and opened it, unfolded the kerchief, and gazed through the glinting diamond particle into a stream of fond memories. Three generations of mother-daughter love swirled around this antique ring.

Surprisingly, the silver band looked good, stronger than it seemed before. I said to myself, "I'd love to wear this, just for today. But it doesn't go with anything. It's kind of plain. It would look ridiculous on my finger."

Well, I was the one, of course, the Queen of Ridiculous. What had I become that I felt I shouldn't wear my grandmother's and mother's ring? And what had I feared in not wearing it in the first place? That I would lose this precious keepsake? That I could not hold on, control? Jewelry is created primarily as a display of affection. Why not let it out of its box? Its simple beauty lay confined and unappreciated, out of the light, not allowed to shine forth.

The parallels startled me. I was the ring. My marriage was the box. Sara was the ring. Her overinvolved mother tidying up her room was the box.

"Let go," I thought. "Allow her to be. And be yourself, while you're at it."

Be yourself. Become everything you are.

I certainly needed my own advice. I put on the ring. It looked plain and ridiculous. I loved it.

The next day I went to a neighborhood jeweler, and by the end of the afternoon he had soldered new silver onto the band. Now it was sturdy and safe. I slipped it on my finger. The crystal chip winked in the sunlight.

Guarding the Garden

During the last year of my marriage, before the pressure cooker of our relationship popped, my husband and I attended a medical congress back east. One night we were invited to an elegant dinner in a fancy Boston restaurant.

It was decorated like a library. Hundreds of bookcases lined the dark velvety walls, creating an aura of history. I felt like I should whisper or tiptoe around. Ten people, all hungry, a conglomerate of intellectuals and eccentrics, sat at a rectangular table covered with white linen and crystal. A very dignified couple, highly respected for their accomplishments in their fields of expertise, sat at the head. They had been married twenty-five years, and I was interested in observing their interaction.

Richard, the husband, ordered last. He took a long time deciding on his main course. He hesitated, then said, "Roast lamb, please."

Everyone stopped talking. I guess people paused to hear his decision. Suddenly, his wife said, in a tone that made me straighten up in my seat, "But, dear, you don't like lamb."

He responded sweetly, but with no equivocation, "I don't like *your* lamb."

The silence was palpable. No one moved. I think the whole restaurant stood still. It seemed that way.

Finally someone ventured a joke and the discomfort passed. Perhaps Richard's wife took a few extra minutes, but soon she resumed her decorum.

I wondered what happened when they returned home that night. How his statement fared with her, after all those years.

I really admired the dignity she demonstrated. It was visible proof of her respect for their unity. That she had said, "Dear, you don't like lamb" did, however, suggest she had a personal stake in her husband's choice of food. Somehow, his preference jeopardized the private picture of what she felt was suitable.

Each of us is given a spiritual plot of ground, a special section of the grand landscape of life. It is our garden, our business, our potential for grandeur. What we do with it, how we tend to the seeds we choose to cultivate, demonstrates our growth.

We sometimes look into another's garden and see weeds or an untended spot. Untended by our standards. We begin to toil and labor in his garden as well as our own.

Richard's wife had obviously been tending portions of her husband's garden for years, taking what he planted and shaping it into a topiary of her own making.

One reason we meddle with the spirit of another is a reluctance to take an honest look at ourselves. It's much easier to tell a companion what is important, how to fix his mess, the mistakes he has made, the correct course of action he should take.

Whenever the view elsewhere is tempting, take a moment to regard yourself. Look closely for the same annoying weeds you spot across the fence. Don't be surprised if you've neglected your own affairs while scrutinizing another's.

When fervency to control gets a grip, when we feel the burning need to supervise, a quick trip back to our personal patch of garden is advised. This is our spot, our domain, our nurturing space that needs attention.

Loved ones flourish when we do this. We develop ourselves much faster as well.

I come to these words of advice through hindsight. If I'd understood some of my own lessons as they revealed themselves, in my control over Sara and my being controlled by my husband, I might have acted differently.

And I tell the restaurant story because I prefer not to belabor the painful details of my own. But what happened between those two people is the final chapter of my marriage writ small.

All the bewilderment and frustration that had built inside me for so many years finally came out. Once I said to my husband, "I want a divorce," once I had made my large, bold rebellion, the recriminations began to fly.

Sometimes the response to someone's meddling in your garden for so long is to leap bitterly into his. This certainly seemed to be the case with that couple at dinner. And it occurred in the early negotiations for my divorce settlement, with my husband and I both hiring saber-toothed lawyers to defend us in the tough fight ahead.

What humans can do to one another is abominable. We're like ax murderers to those we love. We chop them with hurtful observations, cut them with relentless epithets attesting to their weaknesses, splay them with criticism and painstaking descriptions of their vulnerabilities and shortcomings.

By the time my husband and I had completed the private terrors of our allegations, we no longer lived together.

Counting the Mountain Goats

One of the last things I did before leaving California was go to the Wild Animal Park in San Diego. My husband and I used to visit there often, but now I went alone.

The park, located in the hills outside the city, is a magnificent natural reserve. It comprises an extensive collection of creatures from all over the world. A fifty-minute guided monorail tours through eighteen hundred acres of cultivated territory to observe "wild animals" in captivity. Each scene holds sample species indigenous of the specific landscape. Exhibits include a savanna, a desert, mountainous terrain, and a hidden jungle.

On this day the tram I rode passed the fenced enclosures, and the guide offered fascinating facts on social behavior, diet, and whether the animals had made the "endangered species" list. I thought about how endangered the natural and innocent beauty within me had become.

We soon stopped at my favorite exhibit, a small mountain where tiny goats run, eat, and lounge, indifferent to the endless trainloads of eager tourists watching them.

"There are 28 mountain goats," the guide told us. "Take your time to count them."

An innocent request. How hard could it be to count to 28?

I began, "1, 2, 3, 4."

A little boy sitting next to me started, "1, 2, 3, 4. Mommy, look, a mouse!"

I concentrated, "5, 6, 7, 8, 9, 10."

He started, "1, 2, 3, 4, 5." He counted loud, "6, 7, 8, 9 . . ."

Absent-mindedly, I joined him in cadence, "10, 11, 12."

I got lost. I started again.

The little critters blended into their environment. It was tough to distinguish them from the rocks and bushes. Each time I tried, I failed to find all

28. I usually got to 18 before something happened to make me start again.

When I was little, I loved those activity books with lists of twenty-five objects hidden in intricate designs. Later I bought them for Sara. Some of the items were easy to spot, visible even before you peeked at the list at the bottom of the page. Discovering them enhanced my respect for delicious detail in life. I loved the puzzle, the hunt.

My mother always said, "Count your blessings." I would lie awake at night and review my list of things to appreciate. I collected, counted, and filed away blessings and dreams, and arranged them neatly for handy accounting.

As I got older, day-to-day survival and rote familiarity made life an exercise in numbness. I didn't recognize new blessings or dreams. There were times I descended into a valley perpetually covered with clouds. Negativity camouflaged my surroundings as I counted the hardships, loneliness, and pain. Life led me linearly from experience to experience. Like a leaf floating on a stream, I traveled in an unappreciable continuum.

Now I had risen above the shadows and I began to see things clearly. For the first time in my life I had, through the divorce, taken a course of action in my own direction and on my own behalf. This wasn't selfishness, although friends and relatives perceived it as such. I believed only that I loved life, and in order to grow I had to let this desire flourish. After spending fifty years on the planet, I saw the move as very simple. All of life's decisions are simple, although the complexities that lead to them may be as numberless as thoughts in a day.

I felt exhausted, somewhat anaesthetized by the breakup. But I had no regrets. Nothing about the process saddened me, except that it had taken so long in coming, and the wrangling over the settlement dragged on.

Here on the tram, however, I caught myself doing something I hadn't done since I was a young girl. I was counting my blessings. I was having what I'd later call inbetweens, though subtle ones. Even the little counting boy who kept making me lose count was an inbetween within an inbetween.

But I think the moral of the story is that I kept losing count because that's the nature of blessings: there are so many we always lose count.

The Phoenix

My former husband is an extraordinary man. He is a medical scientist and his contributions in the field of genetic research have impacted thousands of lives for good. I feel honored to have shared his greatness. Sometimes I think it wasn't his domination over my psyche that distressed me so much as the structure of entrapment the marriage represented. He played a role many husbands play. It's been a cultural imperative for men to assume they should take the lead, be the lords of their castles, and that wives exist only to support their lofty pursuits. Most husbands don't understand— or even consider— that a marriage should be a true partnership, decisions made jointly, and that wives' ambitions and dreams equal their own. How typically unbalanced our marriage was. So unbalanced that I felt the only way I could rise to a position of self worth was to leave.

I thought about staying on in California. But for me it had become an environment of such fervent posturing and superficiality, like my marriage, that I decided to move away.

Now I live in a tiny town a few steps from the North Shore of O'ahu in Hawai'i. My life is simple and rural. I can walk to shops, homey shops in small, quaint buildings. There isn't a mall for thirty miles. I hear roosters crow, not just at dawn, but all the time. This is a raw place, teetering in a delicate equilibrium. Many races live next door to each other, blending and sharing and eventually dissolving into a subculture unique to this plot of land. The give-and-take is evident in the foods, clothing, language, and lifestyle. Even the roosters contribute to the drama, hurling themselves into their song without concern for the appropriate time of day.

I love walking in my neighborhood. I think I spotted a possible rooster residence the other day. In the backyard of one of the houses was a row of lean-to structures walled with corrugated iron. On the top of one of the coops perched a colorful rooster. He flapped his wings, elongated his neck, lifted his beak to the sky, and warbled his greeting.

Houses scattered on the outskirts of town are weather-beaten wooden shacks. Some appear to double as small barns. The roofs sag, porch steps are crooked, and all have single-wall construction. Broken-down old cars decorate the yards, accentuated with cracked pottery flower pots, and laundry hanging out to dry. Bright red or orange flowers grow on vines. Untrimmed tree branches hide porches. There's nothing orderly or manicured about this place, nothing like the upscale California suburb I came from.

On my walk I discovered between two tiny "plantation-style" houses a rutted little road just wide enough for a car to drive cautiously down the middle. Bougainvillea and hibiscus flowers of red, pink, yellow, purple, white, and orange hung over the weather-grey, untreated wood plank fences that lined both sides of the lane. While the morning sun gently warmed me and the roosters sang in chorus, I thought about the circumstances that had brought me to such simple wonders.

And *simple* is the key word.

I have replaced the hyperactivity of what some consider a wonderful life— of regal cars, fancy department stores, and high society functions— with the most basic of natural pleasures: the smell of rain descending from green mountains, the watery hiss and crackle of a breaking wave, the red powder of iron-rich dirt on my bare feet.

My intention was never to retreat this far from the life I'd known. It just happened that way. After I came to Hawai'i I relaxed. Perhaps for the first time in my life, I let go.

The old persona I'd created, a caricature of my true self, was a one-dimensional reflection of everything I thought I should be. That entity dissolved.

Like the phoenix, I burned up and began to reassemble as something new. I let the ashes of the past blow away to achieve peace of mind in the present.

In this state of relaxation and transition I had no expectations. Then the inbetweens began to shine through. Interesting. I saw the red coat. I witnessed so many other glaring important little phenomena I had to give them a name. My inbetweens must have been like the first sparks of rejuvenating life that reformed the phoenix, the firebird that rose anew from the ashes of its immolation.

I began to feel myself change.

The Magic Machine

I decided inbetweens were outward manifestations of my inner spark. "La chispa de la vida," the Spanish say: *the spark of life*. Inbetweens reminded me of who I had been as a little girl. I never lost the light of my soul. It had only diminished greatly since childhood, and this new sensation of filling with light— the enlightenment I was experiencing— moved me toward the full restoration of my inner power.

One dandy perquisite of the process was an unassailable sense of independence. I was making it on my own.

Life happens chronologically, but the life of the mind swings like a pendulum through past, present, and future. What went on around me during and after the breakup of my marriage accounted for little of what went on inside. An experience or thought pattern might take me into memories, an inbetween would echo something similar in my past, and all the while I could see how the light streaming into my soul brought lessons with it, turning me into a strong, confident, and happy person. My posture improved. Incredibly, so did my eyesight. I found myself using my reading glasses less often. As things became clearer to me on a metaphysical level, so did they on the physical.

The changes in my mind and spirit took on counterparts in the real world. Everything became a lesson.

For example, I had a slow, uncooperative, aging computer that I'd moved with me to Hawai'i. The commands it called for made me crazy. I never felt we belonged together. We just didn't communicate. I created obstacles to avoid learning how to use it properly. Its capabilities ranged well beyond my needs. It was a Sherman tank.

I needed a Jeep. Something smaller, less complex. Something I could carry with me if I had to move again.   A simple tool that didn't require such incredible effort.

I yearned for a "laptop." Its size was inviting, less imposing than my old clunker. I thought, "When I write my observations about inbetweens, I want to learn how to do more than three things on the computer. I want to carry my work with me. I want to love my computer since I intend to write about love."

So a new laptop came into my life.

I mastered the basics in the guide book, incorporated some wonderful new tricks, and bought a couple of advanced manuals that bolstered my hopes. But I left the old computer hooked up to my printer. I had mastered the printer because someone set it up for me. To unplug it was out of the question.

I couldn't set the old computer aside. Like holding your mother's hand when you're learning to walk, I couldn't detach myself. Instead, I worked a million times harder, learning to copy everything onto a disc, then copy it again onto the old computer to print it out. But my discs wouldn't play leap frog forever. It worked for two days, then a cryptic message bleeped up suddenly on the screen, indicating there was something wrong, "DIFFERENT DENSITIES!"

During the disc transfer I lost four pages of material. I felt sick that night and went to bed sweating. I needed to make a change. The old one had to go. It complicated everything.

Look how convoluted I made things, simply because I kept clinging to that old, aging idea.

Early the next morning, after a sleepless night, I called the Word Perfect hotline. I had to move forward and feel free to write. I needed to reflect the same freedom in my writing. I wanted a little laptop because it implied liberation.

"I should be smart enough to follow simple directions," I thought. "What is a hotline for? They spoon-feed people and field their emergent needs."

Well, I called the company and got Doug on the phone. I told him the whole thing about the laptop, the discs, and holding on to the old computer and printer: my list of complexities.

He listened politely. He didn't seem concerned about finding the remedy. He did say one thing up front. "Bonnie, why don't you just use the new one? Set aside the other computer and hook the laptop to your printer. It'll be much simpler."

I don't know what I was expecting. I needed help and that's what Doug offered. But when the truth hit I felt foolish.

I tried stalling a bit. "Well, I'm not at all mechanically minded. I might not be able to figure out the printer hook-up and maybe I should have the old one as back-up."

He said, "You already have plenty of back-up with the discs. You don't need another computer."

He was on to me. All of my fears about dealing with this machine were exposed. I said, "It's bad, Doug. I can't even set my clock radio."

His next remark settled me down. Compassion came through. He said very softly, "My wife is like you. We have a baby girl. She's ten months old and she loves to play with the buttons on the television. She pushes them all the time. My wife has to call me to get the picture back the way it's supposed to be."

We stayed on the phone for another hour. He guided me through the incredibly easy process of moving the old computer to its new, honored position on the floor of my closet.

Then I took the cable that led from the printer and plugged it into the jack that had a picture of a printer above it. Next, I found the disc that came with the printer, loaded it into my laptop and pressed "PRINT."

The machines, working together, dot-matrixed the first ten pages of my reminiscences.

We did it. Me, Doug, my laptop, and my printer. What a team!

I don't do fancy stuff. Thank goodness graphs don't fit anywhere in my manuscripts because I can't go that far yet. I did, however, effect a small, significant change.

This computer exercise reminded me of learning to drive a stick-shift, and I think that was my immersion course after my move: learning to master new hookups, learning to shift gears.

I remember how tough it was in high school that term I took Driver Education. Half the football team watched from the Auto Mechanics classroom as we beginners practiced in the parking lot. Each time my car lunged forward, the boys (all twenty-four of them) rewarded me with rousing cheers and grunts, clapping and howling.

Kermit Ambrose, our instructor, told us to relax. "Think about one thing at a time. Keep your actions fluid. Focus on slowly easing the clutch out as you gently apply pressure to the accelerator."

I spent entire class periods chugging around the lot, trying to put distance between me and the building. I was never out of the football boys' sight, and the wind carried their hoots everywhere.

It's remarkable I learned to drive at all. Eventually, the forward fluid movement Mr. Ambrose talked about became natural, but it took weeks, and my mistakes were painfully apparent.

Change demands concentration. It means leaving a place of learned expression that is not expansive, and rearranging thought patterns to accommodate a higher perspective, a better understanding of life's lessons.

I confess that even with the help of inbetweens, my growing command over the psychological machine hasn't been without its different densities and grinding gears. Old patterns of belief arise, and I exhibit occasional jerks of confusion.

It's not always easy, but Mr. Ambrose was right. "Focus and keep your movements fluid."

And so I am well on my way. I wipe off the old, caked-on gunk of poor attitudes to see their relationship to bygone pain and disappointment, and I find a place of equilibrium and spark. My window is clean.

I remind myself that if babies didn't love to learn, we'd all be crawling.

Balancing on Boulders

Learning to shift into my new life brought catcalls much like those from the critical football players mocking my driving. After the divorce some of the judgments made by loved ones forced me to examine my reasons for leaving. People interpreted my actions from a limited view. They saw the filtered reality my husband and I offered to the world. They saw the hurt I caused, the "selfishness" and "irresponsibility."

Were their perceptions true? Was this me?

All my life I've tried to please. I even convinced myself that other people's opinions were superior to my own.

Was my departure an egotistical, narrow excuse for a superficial mind to indulge itself?

These thoughts whirled around in my head at Christmas time, away from most of my family. I accepted the blame. A whole bunch of people dear to me were in utter disarray because I had acted on my individuality. The family extends from here to Israel, from Finland to Italy. No one really understood. My actions bewildered them.

Could I make this determination for myself and trust it would be beneficial?

Like many women of my generation, when I spoke my mind, the words bubbled out not as a form of direct communication, but in a dialect of soft persuasion in deference to my husband's position. Rarely did I choose to be severely honest, and then I usually took so long that my conversation deteriorated into defensive or reactionary comments. I had no balance. My husband expressed himself with impunity. I gave him that freedom. I was glad to. I just forgot to take the same liberty.

"Was I selfish in leaving?" I asked myself. "Could I have stayed? Were my critics right in saying I fled from duties?"

No. I handled the decision as well as I could at that stage of understanding. I did everything with an allegiance to duty.

I bear no shame in this.

For months I remained stuck in my internal dialogue of justification. Then one afternoon I looked out my window toward the ocean and recalled a man-made, lava rock jetty built to calm the water in the small harbor nearby. It seemed remote, different from the protective green foliage I usually encountered on my constitutionals. I decided to take a walk. I put on shoes and thick white socks, feeling a twinge of nervousness about the unknown turf ahead, but hopeful I could break this mind lock.

I walked by the beach park, passed a small marina of fishing boats, stepped onto the big lava boulders and picked my way to the very end of the jagged gangplank of stone. Giant waves hit the rocks and trickled in thin streams through the cracks in the wall.

When I got to the end I stopped, turned, and looked back toward shore.

From where I stood, I saw a panorama unparalleled in my memory, an incredible glimpse of glory. Green velvety hills rolled over onto each other with the movement of the wind rippling through sugar cane fields. Little dollhouses dotted the countryside. Misty cloud puffs settled softly along the craggy tops of the peaks of a wide, luscious mountain range. Waves crashed next to me with spray spouting up at least twenty feet in the air, while small sailboats napped lazily in their slips. A handful of surfers waited for a perfect wave. Smooth, tanned bodies stretched in the sun.

I saw the rugged and tamed, the sublime and aggressive, side-by-side, and I balanced these extremes and thought of the paradox of selfishness versus self-preservation. At what point does the need to break free to heal from an outgrown attachment become a selfish venture?

I don't know how long I stood entranced before I remembered to breathe. I opened my mouth, gulped the sea air, and almost fell. I swooned like a nineteenth-century lady with a corset too tight. I cried. My tears weren't of sorrow or pain, but of gratitude for the recognition of this infinite beauty.

Such are the moments of inbetweens, when I'm taken over by a childlike wonder of life's ordinary marvels.

A faint mist of rain tickled my face. The orange light of the setting sun filtered through wind-borne droplets and turned them golden, like pixie dust. As I stood on the jetty, stabilizing my position, I opened my arms to the elements, faced the sun, and released the judgment of all those people who felt confusion because of me.

Then I watched a rainbow ascend and arch in the gold-washed grey evening sky.

Rosy Cheeks and Lederhosen

My daughter had reached her third year of college, and was studying in Vienna. During her winter holiday she passed the national Austrian ski exam and became a certified ski instructor. In the Alps she met people from all over the world.

One day as I worked on my laptop, trying to shape a storm of random thoughts into a few calm sentences, I decided to telephone her. I didn't really think I would reach her, but a strong urge compelled me.

She picked up the phone (twelve hours away), and her voice struggled to say hello. She was sobbing.

"What's wrong, Sara?"

"Oh, Mom," she said. "Something terrible happened today. This morning I taught a group of mixed nationalities, three Israelis and one German." She stopped to blow her nose. "We had no problem with the language. Everyone spoke English. One of the Israelis, a woman, was afraid of heights and had real trouble with the downhill portion of our lesson. I decided to confine the group to an easy area on the lower part of the mountain. The two Israeli men really grumbled. But I'm responsible for the safety of the entire group, so I held fast to my decision."

"That sounds wise," I said.

"When we got back to the ski school to pay for the day," Sara continued "the Israeli men refused to give me the full amount. They said they hadn't been challenged enough. Our director, an Austrian, handled their complaints. When they left he spewed out a litany of angry, racial slurs, calling the two men all kinds of names. He got angrier by the minute. "I'm so humiliated and outraged," she said through tears. "The worst part is, I didn't tell him I'm Jewish!"

"Oh, Sara!"

She began to sob again. She said, "Mom, I'm really furious. I felt his hatred for them, and my own for him. How can I face him tomorrow? How can I look him in the eye again knowing he expressed those appalling feelings?"

I listened quietly. I searched my thoughts, as a mother, for something consoling to say, something that would soothe her heart and help her grasp a broader vision. I searched my thoughts, as a human being, for some hope.

I'm appalled when ANYone, ANYwhere, of ANY nationality thinks fanatic things about another member of the human family.

It came to me. "Sara, think of him as a little boy with rosy cheeks and lederhosen. Think of him before he ever heard any criticisms, before he had a chance to know anything except the wonderful things children know. Think of him before he knew anything about hatred. Imagine him like that."

She stopped crying and said, "Oh, Mom. You're so funny. But that works. I can see him. I love that little boy. He's so sweet with his rosy cheeks and lederhosen. He's so innocent." And she laughed.

The tearful trance had broken, at least for the moment. Sara's prejudice of this man's prejudice stopped. It transformed itself into a tender glimpse, an inbetween.

This doesn't change the reality of the concentration camps, but for one person, for one moment, it stopped ugliness and horror. Sara won't forget the time when she felt compassion toward someone who clearly expressed loathing for her collection of relatives.

She successfully disassembled previous history. She dismantled gossip and unbelieved a most conspicuous component of reality. She refused to accept that anger needs to be returned. She disavowed the collective opinion that "you cannot love an intolerant, narrow-minded person."

Love does more than just neutralize. It takes negativity and replaces it with a feeling of well being.

Sara felt the benefits of a shift in perspective. She told me a few days later that she saw the director getting out of his car and trudging through the clean, white snow in the Tyrolean Alps on the way to work. "I envisioned him as a rosy-cheeked little boy in lederhosen and loved him unconditionally," she said. "You know, Mom, it's possible to love people if you stop hating them first."

She spoke to the director later about how they could demonstrate respect for all the nationalities the school served. She never mentioned her heritage, but let her fresh, child-like view of innocence make a difference.

Share the Wealth

Inbetweens and their effects became my daily companions in life. As I came to identify and understand them by— recognizing them, the ability to create them, the realization inbetweens were a power source, and the turning of that energy outward from myself— I witnessed more extraordinary manifestations of their magic.

One day in a local coffee shop, I noticed a tall, distinguished man. He sat by himself, reading the morning paper at the corner table. I could tell he was native born, native to Hawai'i. Black strands peppered his neatly-combed wavy white hair. His mustache made him look like a gallant lord. As he slowly lifted the coffee cup to his lips, white steam rose in sharp contrast against his dark, tanned skin.

I watched him for a while before I leaned over and said, "I must tell you I've lived in Hawai'i for only a few months and I think your homeland is beautiful. I assume you've lived here all your life?"

He gave me a stern look. "Foreigners dilute ethnic purity," he said.

"I beg your pardon, " I said. "Foreigners?"

"It's people like you who have taken our sacred land and put up McDonald's. My brother calls it the Californication of Hawai'i."

Stunned and hurt by his words, I turned around in my seat and sat silently, sipping my coffee. Then I went to the counter and bought him a freshly baked chocolate-chip cookie. I returned to my table and reached out and placed the cookie next to his paper.

He looked up, surprised.

"You need a cookie," I said.

He turned his eyes down.

"And it isn't people like me," I said. "That kind of fast-food assembly-line architecture is ruining the mainland too. It seems like everything that's quaint and non-intrusive is being bulldozed away and replaced by boxes. And where there used to be marshes and meadows there are miles and miles of shopping malls. Have you been to the mainland?"

"Yes," he muttered. "I think it's ugly."

"Not all of it," I said. "Have you seen the Rockies? Or been through the farmlands in the Midwest and South? Have you seen the Atlantic coast? There are places there that remind me of parts of O'ahu."

"I like the Rockies," he admitted.

"I love it that the mountains are so very high, " I said, "and when you're that far up you can look out over prairies and hills for a hundred miles. And the snow, the crisp air, and snowflakes! Have you ever held a snowflake in the palm of your hand and seen the crystal in it?"

"No, I've never done that," he said. "I was there in the summer."

"You've never seen snow?"

"No," he said.

"Well, I'm envious that you have that to look forward to. If you're there when the snow is falling, catch a snowflake and take a good look. Every crystal is different, but they each have six points. Remember that when you look at them the first time."

He shrugged.

"I don't know what to compare it to here," I said. "Maybe those little sparkling things on the beach at night. You know the little blue glowing bits that wash up on the sand? They aren't like snow crystals, obviously, but I experienced the same thrill when I saw them."

He smiled wistfully. "Phosphorescence," he said. "When I was a small kid my father would take us out, and the whole tide line made a line of blue like that," he said. "There must have been millions of those little sparks like necklaces on the sand. The water was full of phosphorescence then. We'd scoop some up and put them in a jar like a blue lantern, enough light to read by."

"Wow," I said. "Which beach was this?"

"Ka'ena side."

"I've been out there."

"It's not the same now," he said.

"I hiked all the way to Ka'ena Point," I said. "It was cloudy on the North Shore, but when I looked south, along the leeward coast it was sunny."

The man leaned forward over his coffee and looked purposefully into my eyes. "Ka'ena is sacred," he said. "It's the place Hawaiian souls jump from this life into the spirit world."

I nodded. "I know how that feels."

We talked for a long time. I had persisted in my happiness as Granny Cravens would have done, and I think that, more than anything won him over. I told him how I really felt about his islands, how life here wraps warmth around your body, heart, and soul, and calls you in for a hug.

Whatever I said or did, something softened him. He used my inbetweens to collect his own. He finally picked up the cookie and took a bite. And we became friends.

As I thought back on this wonderful encounter I could see all four phases of inbetween magic at work. It doesn't always dawn on me I've glimpsed an inbetween until sometime after the event. But I realized the man himself had a glow, in spite of his caustic remarks when we first began talking. I think he'd allowed the spirit of joy within him to be encased in unfounded prejudice. Without even thinking, I had created an inbetween for him with the cookie, and more with my memories and then his memories. His hard facade fell away. I had projected my growing inner light, and the more I projected the more it returned to me through him.

The phases can and do overlap. Sometimes I might simply recognize an inbetween (like a Polaroid picture, one quick snap and it appears instantly). Other times I will pause and meditate on it. Or I may practice my positive attitude in the face of strong negativity, as I did this day, just as my Granny would have done. Occasionally the four phases combine, and when that happens there's usually a big lesson coming.

I believe I learned this day the principle of GIFT. Giving is what the energy flow of inbetweens is all about. Nothing is ours to keep. Everything is ours to take in, and let go. If we hoard life's riches, in the form of memories, money, unworn jewelry, knowledge, power, affection, toys, food, art, clothing, land, water, air— anything created by God or man—we turn inward and the spiritual and material plenitude is wasted. Greed poisons the body and soul. Life's abundance (and that is all life is: abundance) is meant to be shared.

If we love something and share it with others, we double our appreciation. What we find to be good we can keep and give away at the same time. For if we hide what we find, its luster fades in our hearts, and its enchantment is forgotten.

A week before I was due back in California to attend the final discussion on my divorce settlement, I felt a wave of darkness engulf me. I didn't want to return to the incivility I felt so fortunate to have escaped. I would be expected to pick up the fight again and be really tenacious if I wanted a fair portion of my husband's and my joint property.

I found myself in the coffee shop again late one morning, and I bought a chocolate-chip cookie. I walked to the outside tables and sat alone. There were no customers, but I wanted to be without distractions. A breeze rattled the leaves of a nearby eucalyptus tree. I drank my coffee and ate my little treat.

Sometimes you really do need a cookie.

Bunnies in the Sky

That day as I was eating my cookie, my Hawaiian friend appeared again, the screen door from the coffee shop banging shut behind him. I must have looked sullen and determined about my solitude, because he didn't come and sit at my table. But he did move to a chair within my peripheral vision.

I glanced over.

He waved shyly and smiled. How white his teeth were.

I smiled back.

"Care for some company?" he asked.

We chatted for a long while that morning, and we met many times since. I think he likes it that I speak my mind without fear of offending him, because he certainly is imposing; most people probably cower in his presence. We argue a lot, about politics and religion and the vexed state between men and women. I don't know if I can say with confidence that I teach him anything in our exchanges, but I know he teaches me.

One day just prior to my trip to California, we met for coffee again and sat outside. In the deepest part of a very good debate he suddenly said, "Look at that cloud. What does it look like to you?"

The question frustrated me. He was not winning points in our conversation and now he wanted to change the subject.

"All right, fine," I thought. "I'll play along."

I had my back to the sugar cane fields, where he pointed. He insisted I look, so I complied, turning my body around to see the cumulous composition.

There, suspended in an otherwise clear blue sky, was a big, beautiful, completely formed fluffy white bunny. Its remarkably long ears stood at attention. A breeze must have brushed by its face, because I'm sure I saw its nose wiggle.

Our verbal contest, which had been getting hotter by the moment, immediately took a fresh twist.

How could anyone behold such a whimsical creature and not react? The grandeur of that billowy form of downy cuddles propped high in the sky, so soft and luminous, guided our instincts to reach out and receive its gentle tidings.

And then in the clouds beyond emerged more bunnies, or the suggestion of them at least, with rounded backsides, an ear or two poking up, rolling on for miles.

What started out as an imposition, a diversion to an avid debate about upheaval in the world, turned into a soothing interlude of indisputable glory. The argument and discord vanished entirely, and in their place serenity and humor filled the sky.

The gift of these clouds, visible to anyone paying attention, would have been ignored if my friend hadn't made me turn and look.

So twice within days the concept of GIFT had presented itself to me.

When I was little, the phrase "It is better to give than to receive" confused me. I loved receiving. I could think of nothing better. As I grew and began to participate in genuine giving, I understood. Love needs to be shared to expand.

Any evidence of love is a gift: a smile, a thank you, acknowledgement of accomplishments, a pat on the back, a friendly ear for another's sorrows, a bunny in the clouds.

On my flight back to California I determined how tenacious I would be on the divorce settlement: not at all. Before the meeting, I called my attorney and told her I had changed my mind. I would give in at every point. My gift to my husband was to encourage him to give freely only what he wanted to give, only what he thought fair. Not surprisingly, his generosity was mutual. We released our lawyers and decided to mediate the final settlement. What we both expected would be a bitter, lamentable process turned into something wonderful. We are now friends and our healing process continues.

BOOK THREE

Jerusalem,
City of Light

"Ye are the light of the world.
A city that is set on a hill cannot be hid."
Matthew 5:14

Alone

This morning I returned to look at the vines clinging to their nooks and crannies on the little lane near my apartment. They didn't seem possessive about their importance in the bigger picture. They were calm, undisturbed, growing to their fullest potential.

The ramshackle fences with delicate blossoms of color floating through the openings became for me an inbetween.

Fences of pain and disappointment fade slowly, and eventually the flowers of healing adorn the decay.

I used to drive an expensive car and live in a magnificent house that looked like an Italian villa.

I visited friends in foreign places, participated in intellectual conversations, and entertained highly successful people from many career areas.

From the outside I lived the American Dream, and I am grateful for having had such prosperity and rich experiences. But on the inside I felt trapped. And I nearly self-destructed.

I now rent a one-bedroom, ground level apartment month-to-month. I have gathered most of my furnishings from around town. I lease a rusted old car that is covered with dents. Naggi, the leasing agent, attached a sketched-on xeroxed photo of it to the lease agreement. Every possible blemish on the car is dotted with a red pencil and has a pointing arrow. Recently, someone tried to break into the trunk. The burned opening around the keyhole is a new crimson mark on Naggi's drawing. Naggi gets $50.00 for the damage and my trunk doesn't open.

I live on a beach just feet from the ocean and I can look out my sliding door at the Pacific. My social life is limited to local shopkeepers and a few eccentric people who frequent the establishments in this rural town. I have placed myself in another solitary environment: remote, isolated, and detached.

My sister lives an hour away. My mother is in the nursing home near her. My daughter and her new husband moved in down the road from me. They are great sources of love, but they have their own lives.

I don't want to invite pity. I believe we must cultivate love without encroaching on others. I chose these surroundings. I chose this life. What it lacks I have created. The joys and expansion it brings I have also created.

Even in this place of great beauty, with family and love close at hand, I am alone.

So here I sit on Saturday afternoon. I have no plans, nowhere to go, no ideas about what to do. I've read everything in the apartment, TV is boring, and I face the grave realization that "I'm alone."

My arms and legs hardly move. They feel like they're bound with heavy-gauge bungee cord attached to my fingers and toes. I can't imagine stepping forward or even standing up. People have described this feeling as catatonic. That's not it. I am drifting, but stuck. The walls aren't closing in; they're my self-imposed barriers. If I could move, where would I actually go?

Now what?

Before, during, and after the divorce I experienced countless hours of solitude. The word "alone" scared me. I looked it up in the dictionary, and synonyms like remote, detached, and isolated glared out. I checked further and found more hopeful interpretations: unparalleled, unequaled, unique. My favorite is "unique." It's the lovely idea of being rare and distinctive. Finally, at the end of the list, I spotted "original."

There are four white cinderblock walls surrounding me as I sit back to consider my life. It occurs to me "I have a choice." Isn't it strange to recognize something so basic to common sense." I do have a choice. Many choices, in fact. Self-pity is one. Anguish, sorrow, and loneliness are cornerstones I used in the past, but they're words for a victim. And I no longer fit that description. It is time to change the vocabulary.

Slowly, a warm glow pulses through my thoughts, into my body, through my extremities, out to the ends of my elbows, up my neck and into my eyes and ears, and suddenly I can see and hear.

I know that it doesn't matter what I do, where I go, if I go alone or not. Nothing matters but the thought that I am someone, and because I am, I am. To the

Cartesian dictum "I think, therefore I am," I add "I am, therefore I do." Clarity comes for a moment as I see the old pattern of self-doubt I used in the past. What movie should I go to? With whom? How many invitations did I get? How many did I not get? Even if it seems that everyone I know is busy and I'm not, and even if self-pity plagues me, I still know I am, and therefore I *can* do.

I am the creator of my world. I determine outcome. I choose the perspective I use to view life.

What is left when I place another's opinion of who I am above my own? Who can I be when I am a reflection in someone else's mirror?

A quiet voice whispers, "Original. You are an original. You reflect value. You are a creation. Novel. Genuine. Authentic. Unique." That's me, original and unique, alone, the master of my world.

I circle certain words like a hungry shark: endurance, resolve, courage, patience, gratitude, clarity. Standing in front of starkness with nowhere to go tests my definition of these qualities. Real worth and real value are determined by me. Qualities I possess belong to me. These are the inbetweens that bind my being. They are the substance I use for expression. I share them every minute of every day, in every act I do, and with every acquaintance I meet. They are not determined by what others reflect. They make me unique, different, and apart. My authenticity allows me to contribute to the magic of life in ways no other is capable.

Me, alone.

I select my feelings and generate emotions.

I appreciate privacy now. Most of the time I don't see myself as detached, or anything remotely negative. Sometimes the old views haunt me, but when they do, I return to my ongoing thesis: "Love exists, even if only in tiny doses, an inbetween or two, here or there."

As inbetweens appear, I stuff them into every nook and cranny possible until there's no room left for doubt.

Maybe I'll have to work this out again tomorrow, or next Saturday when I look at the cement walls, but I know now the thoughts I need are here, pounding in my head, pulsing through my heart.

Taking time "alone" gives me a chance to reflect real worth by honoring the value of who I am. It doesn't matter where I live, how many friends I accumulate in my life, or how many social engagements I attend. I had it all and was alone. I gave it all up and became all I need.

A Rainbow of Galoshes

After my trip back from California I collected inbetweens with an exuberance Miss Paisley would have graded A. I recorded them and categorized them. Each meant something different.

Here's one:

On a narrow side street, near the center of town, tucked snugly beneath shady trees, is a little white wooden church.

I often pass it on my walks.

The steeple, topped with a cross, forges through the shadows of a grove of big mango trees. In the back of the church is a small one-room day care center with a fenced playground. Three wide steps lead to a set of double glass-paned doors, and some mornings, if I'm lucky, I see the two and three year olds, ushered into school by their parents.

On the top stair are tiny shoes, pairs of glossy-bright, comic-book-colored plastic boots lined neatly in front of the door. They are cute rain galoshes in yellow, turquoise, pink, red, and royal blue.

They look so tidy, each pair clearly meant to hold two little feet attached to a very small person who adores the galoshes more than anything in the world. Someone understood the value of each pair of these little shoes and took the time to lovingly arrange them.

The old rustic church and the rainbow of galoshes provide a blink of innocence, a lasting impression that makes me feel warm and adds a giggle to my life.

It's magic to recognize love. Tiny gestures of care, like the organized arrangement of the little boots on the preschool step, are just small demonstrations, colorful twinkles life gives us. When we see them and recognize their significance, we take in the feeling and it radiates from us.

The ability to recognize and express love is the measure of success in life because it reflects our thoughts and intentions.

If we are clouded with anger, anger surrounds us. If we focus on happiness, we see it in everything and everyone, and are surrounded by it.

The way we perceive our world, through loving eyes or anger, reflects the filter we have chosen to view our reality.

It takes an ongoing commitment to find love in instances where it's not readily apparent. Our choice is either to let things that seem negative rule our emotions, or to look deeper for the hidden meaning and find understanding.

I look for love expressing itself in every experience I encounter and in every relationship. I love the salt-laden tropical air, flocks of birds soaring in magical formations, ghostly mists that sweep and feather over the soft green mountains. It makes my day when a cashier in the local grocery store is cheerful. I love listening to preschoolers chatter and squeal on the playground. I love the rainbow of galoshes.

The more love I see, the more I have to express.

When things are disturbing I look around for demonstrations of love and find them everywhere. It can be as easy as looking into a school yard on a morning walk, for the smallest glimmer of love can shine across a chasm of difficulty.

Latitude of Love

Cars blend into each other in the distant shimmer of heat. The air conditioner pumps hot air. The small pickup truck next to you has twenty speakers, all set on bass. Your windshield and your chest shiver in the vibration of unintelligible rap music.

The temperature is 99°, humidity 95%. It's typically hot for August. Heat and sweat melt your patience.

Summoning what's left of your sense of humanity, you note the budding tremors of rage. Calm is out of the question. You are blocked. Your focus narrows to a pinhole view of the external stimulation. Turmoil consumes your inner spaces. Reality blurs and every fiber in your musculature fights to control the building anger.

Heat, upon tension, upon frustration, upon helplessness, inching in traffic, spiraling through the range of negative emotion, an irrational, untamed animal slowly begins to take shape. Hairy-knuckled claws wrap tightly around the steering wheel. Perspiration drips from the beast's hunched form.

This scene repeats itself daily in the afternoon rush hour, the hurried life of deadlines and schedules, the limited realm of structured activity. Confined to a life out of balance, most of us work in an environment tipped to the negative, leaving little room for solitude and peace.

We lament the past, rush through the present, fantasize about the future, and constantly regret the lack of time we have for ourselves. But if our hopes were put into one giant cauldron and boiled down, we'd find a thick stock of common sensibility, peace in the midst of trauma and confusion, calm in situations that disturb.

We're all joined in a search for that level of balance that neutralizes events of discord. We pine for the "peaceful times" and then we pursue this bliss by mapping out make-believe settings suitable for tranquillity to exist. Our efforts work toward recognizing the goal, but fail to sustain the magic.

The calm we seek is hidden within.

Parallel lines of latitude surround the globe. Navigators use them to discern location. They are fixed, steadfast tools.

Find your own private latitude, your balance line. Part of yourself is like the fulcrum on a teeter-totter that remains stable, unchanged by movement around it. This place is protected from worldly horrors, protected from criticism, from other people's confusion or invasion. It is not stubbornness, or rigidity, or self-righteousness, or judgment in disguise. This is the very soft and gentle part of yourself, what is meek, humble, grateful. It is the best idea of harmony and peace and love one can fathom, your greatest concept.

Nothing about it suggests grandiosity, like seeing your name in lights at Times Square. It's much softer than that. You know this place. You know it when you pick up a small baby, when you give your seat away on a crowded bus, when you hand your child an ice cream cone and notice her smiling eyes, when you give someone a greeting card at work for nothing special. You especially know this place when you do something good, and nobody knows you did it.

This is the lovable you, the you that you love most.

Even if we are bombarded continuously by a sense of hopelessness, locked into the harried existence of a life out of our control, we can look at momentary oppositions as hidden opportunities to reach a higher thought.

The compass needle is love. It sounds trite. Most people question their ability to express this feeling in their lives, but without it tranquillity cannot be imagined, much less attained.

I recently watched a friend go through the process of identifying her latitude of love. She didn't consciously see it happening, but we discussed it much later on the telephone.

Sue came to Hawai'i for a ten-day visit. She left California exhausted from a hectic job and hassled by the advent of busy winter holidays coming too soon.

I was getting organized to move into a new apartment, so she spent much of her time alone. She snorkeled, collected shells, took walks, read books. We had great conversations, but she enjoyed the solitude and developed a new sense of serenity. The calmness she gained bubbled up from within.

She mentioned one day how much she loved watching her husband pray. She used words like "reverence" and peacefulness" to describe the special characteristics she saw in him at these select moments.

"It touches me deeply," she whispered, as we drove along the coast. I glanced at her face and realized that she was expressing the same reverence.

Sue reached a position of peace in those ten days. She told me on the telephone weeks later, "I don't know what happened there, but it returned with me and it has stayed ever since."

The awareness of her husband's grace was the inbetween she used to find her balance point. She recognized it from other angles, so when she was ready, it simply appeared and gave her direction.

She effected her own healing.

If we can imagine something, then it is possible to achieve. Thinking makes it real. Work makes it happen. An unchanging latitude of love balances our beliefs and creates the harmony we seek.

Diamond Depth

I have two diamond stories to tell.

When Sara graduated from college I gave her the most enduring keepsake I could think of: the diamond-chip ring that Mom had passed on to me. "There'll be bigger and brighter diamonds in your future, sweetheart," I told her. "Perhaps they'll be mounted in gold. But this one carries lifetimes of love."

Now four generations of women, four seekers and lovers of light, have worn this small spark on their fingers.

Sara became engaged soon after, to a lovely young man named Jeff. I kept one other diamond ring in my jewelry box, my engagement ring from Sara's father. I held on to it all these years waiting for just such a purpose. Jeff had recently finished law school and couldn't afford the diamond he wanted for his fiancée. I asked him if he would like to have my diamond to give to her. Sara loves her father dearly, and the diamond represents the love that brought her into the world; it was only right that she should wear it.

When the jeweler showed us the removed and freshly cleaned stone, I held it up to a lamp and examined the facets. Free of the setting, it seemed larger, more intricate, and— although this might sound odd— filled with new purpose.

I thought how like diamonds we are, God's treasures.

A virgin diamond is pulled out of a mine. We are born. Like jewelers, we take this misshapen crystallized stone and carve it into who we become.

Diamonds are difficult to transform. Some of us make one or two cuts and see the world through those limited perspectives, refusing to investigate other facets. A single-cut vantage point allows no counterbalance for light to penetrate. Like looking into a flat, shallow surface, there is no depth, no expanse. The more character traits we explore, the more beautiful and rare the diamond becomes. We bring out the "fire," the luster, the exquisite range of who we are.

Living a life using anger, jealousy, prejudice, control, and greed as motivation creates a constant belief in lack. We don't have enough money, friends, understanding, or freedom. We look out from the darkness of our shallow emotional prisms, unable to move or see, blinded to the sparkle of life and bound by the need to be right or the best or accepted. It soon becomes impossible to love or be loved to our satisfaction. We forget that we need to consider our own lives first, see the magnitude there, expand our awareness of what's good, and release ourselves to explore new facets of our being.

We need to chisel away the dark outer shield of emotions that keep us groping in a dim, self-limiting existence, and polish the rough sections with understanding and insight.

If we learn the skills of good jewelers we are able to add new facets continually.

My life is a constant exercise in learning. I use inbetweens to remember the good and focus on expanding the best parts of myself. I've finally learned that people's judgments have nothing to do with who I am or what I do, and I refuse to pressure others with bold insertions of my opinion.

These lessons have given me the magic I need to stand on my own with confidence. I am the creator of my world. I've begun to see the "fire" and depth of the strong, clear multi-faceted diamond that I am.

And as I explore my potential, I'm filled with the entire spectrum of colors that radiate pure light.

There are treasures in life, those things that we normally think of as treasure: silver and gold, emeralds and diamonds. But ordinary things may shine as brilliantly and enchant us even more.

The question is not how to acquire these gifts, but merely to open our eyes and see them. And it is our responsibility alone to make of ourselves the shining treasure we are meant to be.

Building a City of Light

The first time I heard about Jerusalem it was a place on a map. I'm not born of Jewish heritage or any other specific religious group. Life experience brought Jerusalem into my path through marriage.

I love Israel. During my last marriage my husband and I made several trips to the Holy Land, and every time I went it seemed there was some new astonishment to behold.

On one of our trips we visited Hellig, a close friend who was involved in establishing new settlements on the West Bank. He drove us to the foot of a mountain where we saw hundreds of men and women working side by side to clear an expansive tract of land. A scorching hot midday sun dictated the chosen attire: T-shirts, shorts, sandals, and bandannas. The large graveled area was divided into parts. Each person toiled over a small section to break up the dirt and remove the rock and debris. Some of them used regular shovels while others held large, cumbersome electric drills, but all engaged in a unified effort, individually working to perfect each portion for the good of the greater whole.

The dark soil absorbed the heat of the sun and reflected it into the faces of the workers. They labored and they sweat to build their city. I was surprised with the ethnic range of the people, from dark-skinned to olive, with a number of towheads represented. All looked enraptured, and when we pulled up I half expected them to be singing.

Still, the job seemed overwhelmingly oppressive and absolutely huge. It was exciting to watch them dedicate themselves to a "conscious endeavor," but it looked like an impossible feat to me.

I'd been living in Hawai'i for almost two years— thinking I had learned all I could about inbetweens and simply trying to apply their lessons to all I did— when I overheard someone in the market say "Israel." The word chimed for me. Israel. Israel. I stood in the produce section. I held an orange in my hand, and suddenly it seemed to radiate its color like a small, cool sun. And I recalled the oranges of Israel, in the markets there, and growing on trees at a moshav.

"I have to go to Israel," I said to myself.

It was to be a dream journey.

I contacted Hellig. He met me at the airport. "Before we go anywhere else," I told him, "I want to see how the settlement is coming along."

"Of course," he said with a proud smile. "Then I will take you on the grand tour."

It had been several years, but I foolishly assumed there would be little headway made by the settlers, perhaps a few low buildings, a road or two. What I saw was a miracle. We walked through bustling streets. Where there had once been flat, rocky, sweat-sprinkled ground there rose towering housing complexes. Children played in the school yard. Cars and bicycles made their way through a crowded downtown area. We stopped for coffee and watched the magnificence of the Israelis' accomplishment. The good they expressed was in the achievement, not the politics of that torn land. They worked collectively to create a community, individual effort multiplying itself into a common reality.

My joy was second hand. I didn't do a thing to help. In fact, I doubted it could be done. But I felt so grateful that I'd witnessed this cooperative endeavor. It demonstrated man's recognition that miracles can be accomplished if we work together.

I remember thinking, "Well, here's an inbetween. This whole city is an inbetween."

I began concocting deductions from the experience, little realizing that my ideas were preparing me for a soon-to-come climactic inbetween, which would propel me into the fifth phase of my understanding.

The abstract was about to become real, and as incredible as a sky full of shooting stars.

But first I had to set my observations of the new city with a broader scheme of the human race.

I pondered the evidence of hard work that surrounded me, and how we work separately to create personal realities that reflect our beliefs and attitudes. Most of the time we do this unaware of the consequences upon the collective whole.

We are all connected. Every little thing we do affects others. If we work in a negative attitude, the people influenced by our projections reflect negativity back to us, creating darkness. The darkness can swell to fill entire landscapes as more and more people reflect the anger. When humanity realizes this principle of connected interaction, it is possible for us to evolve into beings with spiritual peripheral vision. Our energies then magnify, and we will feel and contribute consciously to the good of all.

Confucius said, "Man is at birth by nature good." Recognition of our innate goodness and the knowledge of our relationship with the earth, the animals, and humanity is all we need to create an environment of harmony. We look for goodness and love, recognize it, project it, and watch the light ripple through the matrix of relationships we encounter.

Maybe we can't do this all the time at first. Just sometimes, with some people, in some situations. But if each of us clears our space of unwanted negative debris, we can together build a city of light.

Tinkerbell Jerusalem

My plane had arrived at Ben Gurion Airport early in the morning, and Hellig and I stayed almost till noon at the settlement. "Now I want to show you some things," he said. "Then we will end our afternoon with a spectacular vision."

"I'm tired," I said. "Can't we go to the hotel?"

"Ah, Bonnie. Where we are going will refresh you!"

We drove out through the countryside in a circular tour that would bring us back to Jerusalem before dark. We passed Bedouin tent settlements and a green oasis that shone like an emerald on the wheat-colored desert sands. We traveled through scorched plains and desolate brown hills. As we came over a rise, we saw the bluish-grey water of the Dead Sea stretching to the horizon.

Hellig said, "I am taking you for a swim."

The road meandered down to the water, and the air scorched everything. It was very hot. We parked near a row of showers and dressing rooms.

"Swimming in the Dead Sea will make you feel heavy and light at the same time," Hellig told me. "It is a baptism of physical sensations."

He was a soft-spoken man. Each sentence seemed measured, each word carefully selected. I couldn't wait to experience the feeling of opposites colliding and blending together.

Hellig said, "It's important that you shower after the swim."

"Why?" I asked.

He smiled. "You will see."

I put on my bathing suit and walked to the beach. The water lay absolutely still, with only an occasional rise tempting the flat surface. It was quiet and eerie, nothing like the beaches in California or anywhere else I had been. Tiny waves rippled the shore, barely moving the sand.

The late afternoon sun glazed the water with a golden shimmer. I waded in a ways, quickly noticing the viscous texture, which reminded me of partially congealed Jello. The heavy water didn't allow you to swim. It was more like reclining in liquid goop, making you buoyant, light, suspended. I couldn't believe there was such a place. I kept repeating the name, "The Dead Sea." I felt lifeless, floating in a weighted calm.

We lounged in the water for a while, discussing the salty taste, the warm temperature, and how unique it felt to try to sink and not succeed. Hellig got out first and waited on the beach in the shade of an olive tree. As I walked over to join him, I brushed water off my arm and was surprised to find a thick, slippery film coating my skin.

"Hellig, what is this stuff all over me?"

He laughed and said, "Take a good shower. The salt is very dense in the Dead Sea. When it dries, it cracks your skin, and you itch."

"I feel so heavy."

I drenched myself in the fresh cool water, opening my mouth to clear the salty taste from my palate. I had to scrub the residue; water didn't dissolve it alone.

When I was done and toweled off, I felt exhausted. A combination of jet-lag, the long day, heat from the intense sun, the struggle through the buoyant saline, the crusty salt film, and the cold rinse made me want to sleep.

We loaded the car and made our way up another windy road through vast and austere hills. "I am so beat and thirsty," I said to Hellig, "and all I can think about is taking a nap at the hotel."

Hellig said, "There's water in that bottle at your feet. We'll arrive in Jerusalem at dusk, when the lights go on."

I'd forgotten his promise of a spectacular vision. So the lights would go on. Big deal. I wanted to rest.

We wound higher and higher until we arrived at a small summit parking lot. Hellig stopped the car near a sign that read, "The Mount of Olives."

The sun rested on a hill to the west and slowly descended to a crescent of faded orange.

"Come on," Hellig said. "We are here, and the time is perfect." He motioned for me to join him on a rise to look at the view he had so strategically planned.

I walked across the parking lot, climbed the small incline to the ridge where Hellig stood. I noticed his demeanor, so reverent in the warm breeze, his eyes soft and reflective. I followed his gaze and beheld a wonder, a miracle of golden light.

"Jerusalem," he said.

The ancient city nestled in the valley below my feet, each building in its special spot, as if placed there only to be adored. The aged crenelated wall of the Old City rose along the hills, and beyond were the Dome of the Rock, David's Tower, and the other sacred landmarks. The assortment of pale sand-colored Jerusalem-stone structures blended together, soothing to the eye, beckoning.

While the distant sun cast a gentle glow of rosy tones, I watched a thread of sparkles work its way through the city as lights flickered on. One here, two there, a row of lamps across the way, until hundreds of individual little gold lights twinkled in unison, inviting me to feel their power. Each light glowed for its individual purpose, but all were part of the luminous whole.

"I'm free!" I thought.

Immediately, my longing for rest and comfort disappeared, and a light, airy feeling lifted me into a space of exaltation.

The city of Jerusalem has been here for thousands of years, destroyed and rebuilt several times, layer upon layer, an ancient monument of timeless tiers.

All of the sparkling dimensions of who I am, and hope to become, physically appeared. I saw my parallel pattern of destruction and rebirth and felt a kinship to this magnificent symbol of renewal: my life, a microcosm expressed in Jerusalem, the macrocosm.

Everything faded as I witnessed the unfolding of this spectacle of glory. I had unknowingly prepared myself for this vision atop the Mount of Olives with Jerusalem shining. My philosophical connections earlier in the day and my salty baptism in the Dead Sea allowed me to taste life's clarity as if for the first time.

The gift of this moment, basking in the grandeur of the symbol of eternity, changed my life unalterably.

I returned home to a whole new paradigm for inbetweens. They were no longer in between anything. The darkness had lifted. There was magic everywhere.

One day as I sat in my little apartment during a rainstorm, I noticed a single glistening drop of water on my window screen. It sparkled as the screen moved in the wind.

I looked around the living room at my collection of furnishings and realized that each item ignited a memory or feeling of warmth and love. I felt like a child again, lying under the Christmas tree, the lights like a pine-scented heaven filled with colored stars.

"That's it!" I thought. "That is the feeling. That is what I have been looking for, and I've unconsciously surrounded myself with things that spark the love in me."

I gazed at my daughter Sara's picture and felt my love for her. I looked at a crystal my Granny gave me; I felt it again. I'd discovered tiny glimmers of love that lit my spirit for as long as I could hold on to the memory, and as small as they were they resembled the sensations I felt on the Mount.

I went outside. Everything glowed. Rain-beaded leaves shimmered in the trees. Moths drifted by like little dusty angels. A sunray stabbed through the clouds in a sliver of silver.

It's all here. It's all there. I'd made the mistake in my quest of looking *for* something. Looking for inbetweens. Looking for an answer. Looking for help. Looking for love. Looking for. I should have been looking *at*.

It's all here. If you don't believe it, look around now. Lift your eyes. Do you see it? In the field of your vision, no matter where you are, there is an inbetween, a carrier of spiritual light, sending its healing and comfort to you, its love and beauty.

Everything in my life was connected and I was using my inbetweens to create a harmony for myself, packing every space with the consciousness of love and beauty, like the shimmering ceiling in my childhood attic.

When I first experienced inbetweens, I felt as though some outside force, some angelic being or fairy had sprinkled pixie dust on these objects and people for me to see. But now I know who Tinkerbell is.

When a light is shining, I'm doing the shining. The fairy that bestows light in my life is me.

Then I finally got the whole picture.

If I have inbetweens, so does everyone else. If I can use them to erase negative memories, anger, and pain, so can others. If I can fill my life with glimpses of love and expand them to create a reality of harmony, everyone on the planet is capable of doing the same.

If we all find our own inbetweens and use them to generate love and peace, we will radiate that reality. Then, as we touch others' lives, they will reflect it back to us, just like the lights coming on and blending that evening in Jerusalem.

Inbetweens are Tinkerbell's pixie dust, the memories and childlike sparkles that lift us into flight. Jerusalem is the collection of light, a conscious act for harmony, peace, and love, the attainable goal built with the collection of inbetweens.

The mind's power to create bright new perspectives is limitless.

Tinkerbell Jerusalem, whimsy and eternity, exist side by side, recognized and expressed through the love we manifest.

This is our hope for the future.

With each of us generating and reflecting harmony, illuminated with Tinkerbell's pixie dust, we can combine to create the common enlightenment of the New Jerusalem.

Light

A friend lives on the windward coast of the island of O'ahu where tradewinds blow hard, and sometimes deposit treasures from the sea onto the beach in front of her home. Years ago, Japanese fishing trawlers used glass balls as floats for their nets. Hand-blown green globes were fastened to thousands of pounds of netting to hold the mesh suspended in rough seas. Sometimes, if the nets lay deep enough, the pressure of the ocean pushed water through microscopic fissures in the glass and locked the salty fluid inside. Occasionally, glass balls break free of their woven prisons and float through the turbulent open ocean to Hawai'i.

Early-morning beachcombers delighted in finding these emerald globes, rolling in the shore break or tangled in the flotsam near the hightide mark on the sand.

Some balls still have netting attached to them and barnacles and patches of seaweed crusting their smooth surfaces from years of bobbing travel. These jewels are gathered, scrubbed off, and used to decorate homes and yards. I see them everywhere, hanging from porches, as ornaments in gardens, or in baskets in living rooms.

My friend cut a small hole in the top of a glass ball and stuffed it with tiny white Christmas lights. It took seven strands of fifty lights to fill the ball. When she plugged it in, it shone bright enough to light the whole room.

The image of a clear, green globe traveling alone at the whim of wind and currents, collecting life on its surface, allowing external pressures to push unwanted matter through minuscule openings, represents my attitudes and patterns before I discovered inbetweens.

An inbetween, hidden in a clouded memory by misunderstanding, twinkles like a tiny speck of glitter that flickers in your vision and causes you to look closer. Each discovered inbetween glows from within like a faint wisp of light that edifies the memory it touches.

I wrote down each inbetween to celebrate its importance.

As I took direction from inbetweens, I had to look closely at some unpleasant events of my past to find glimpses of joy and heal the memories. Using these impressions and the knowledge of my potential, I saw the negativity that blocked my progress.

I began to approach my memories and everyday experiences as opportunities to find new perspectives. Collecting "pixie dust" and filling emotionally cluttered nooks and crannies with elevated understanding made the light grow in intensity. Like individual Christmas lights, their glow was subtle; but bundled together in a green glass ball, they shared their light and illuminated the darkness.

Inbetweens clustered into loving thoughts that guided my actions. As I filled with this enlightenment and projected it outward, I recognized more beauty around me and watched magic happen. My external world began to correspond to the growing love within me.

I expanded my field of projection into every moment, in every experience and relationship. I recognized the love in others. When my inner feelings manifested themselves, they were reflected back, and they allowed me to see the power I had to control my life.

We move separately, recognizing our magic, radiating joy, and sometimes taking flight with pixie dust. On our journeys, we light a path for others and spiritually shine in unison with them.

I look everywhere, in everything, to find hidden spots of goodness in my heart to radiate out onto the world. I check my progress by watching what the world reflects back to me, and I find that the more love I send out, the more love returns.

As each of us tends our garden of light, cultivating our memories, and weeding out stagnant beliefs, we project harmony and join the ranks of the enlightened. Like stars, each separately powerful, we can radiate a new magnificent consciousness. A New Jerusalem:

> "Neither do men light a candle, and put
> it under a bushel, but on a candlestick; and it
> giveth light unto all that are in the house.
> Let your light so shine. . . ."

My life's journey thus far has brought me back to a childlike wonder and joy, and I am grateful now for all of it, for all of my experiences: for the pain brought by my morphine-addicted, amnesiac father, and for the tenderness and direction he bestowed upon me; for my mother's misery, and for the lace trimmings she surprised me with; for the dark times with my husbands, and for the blissful marmite-sandwich moments that would make me love them forever; for Granny; for my constantly beautiful daughter; for my own doubts and self-criticism, and for my phoenix-like, Tinkerbell Jerusalem recovery.

I have become a child again. An experienced child, a wise old child.

When I explained the magic of inbetweens to a dear friend of mine, she said, "Oh, just like Wordsworth's 'Intimations of Immortality.'" She gave me the poem, and this is part of it:

> There was a time when meadow, grove, and stream,
> The earth, and every common sight,
> To me did seem
> Appareled in celestial light,
> The glory and freshness of a dream.

. . .Thanks to the human heart by which we live,
Thanks to its tenderness, its joys, and fears,
To me the meanest flower that blows can give
Thoughts that do often lie too deep for tears.

Wordsworth wrote the poem as a recollection of early childhood, when to him everything seemed aglow with a "celestial light." But I think he knew that the celestial light still shines. It simply takes the child in each of us to see it and learn by it.

Inbetweens may be as tiny as giving butterfly kisses, walking barefoot over a shimmering dew-laden lawn, or watching for the green flash of a sunset, but the magic they hold will change your life.

I make it a point to count blessings and search out their hiding places.

I find them in the smell of a gardenia, the touch of a friend's soft hand on my shoulder, a crayon, the smell of wood-smoke on a gentle breeze, a kiss on the cheek from an old acquaintance. Call them blessings, call them gifts, call them inbetweens. However they appear, count them, appreciate them, and keep them close to your heart.

And take time to write them down.

You'll see.

Wynken, Blynken, and Nod

by Eugene Fields

Wynken, Blynken, and Nod one night
Sailed off in a wooden shoe, —
Sailed on a river of crystal light
Into a sea of dew.
"Where are you going and what do you wish?"
The old moon asked the three.
"We've come to fish for the herring-fish,
That live in this beautiful sea;
Nets of silver and gold have we,"
Said Wynken,
Blynken,
and Nod.

The old moon laughed and sang a song,
As they rocked in the wooden shoe;
And the wind that sped them all night long
Ruffled the waves of dew;
The little stars were the herring-fish
That lived in the beautiful sea.
"Now cast your nets wherever you wish,—
Never afraid are we!"
So cried the stars to the fisherman three,
Wynken,
Blynken,
and Nod.

All night long their nets they threw
To the stars in the twinkling foam,—
Then down from the skies came the wooden shoe,
Bringing the fishermen home:
'Twas all so pretty a sail, it seemed
As if it could not be;
And some folk thought 'twas a dream they'd dreamed
Of sailing that beautiful sea;
But I shall name you the fisherman three:
Wynken,
Blynken,
and Nod.

Wynken and Blynken are two little eyes,
And Nod is a little head.
And the wooden shoe that sailed the skies
Is a wee one's trundle-bed.
So shut your eyes while Mother sings
Of wonderful sights that be,
And you shall see the beautiful things
As you rock in the misty sea
Where the old shoe rocked the fishermen three:—
Wynken,
Blynken,
and Nod.

BONNIE KELLEY KABACK

Bonnie lives in Hale'iwa, Hawai'i, a remote town on the North Shore of O'ahu. The serenity and privacy of these surroundings gave her the peace she needed to finish her first book, *Tinkerbell Jerusalem*. And now, she is writing more about the glimpses of joy she sees in life.

THREE MONKEYS PUBLISHING has been pleased to bring you this book. If you are so inspired, we would gratefully receive the gift of *your* "inbetweens."

The cornerstone word for Three Monkeys Publishing is "fun." Fun may be the most serious, earnest, and certain word in the English language. Every child has experienced the purity of this word. It is a presence so real that it can be felt with every nerve ending.

No negatives stick to fun. No meanness, no guilt, no hang ups, no tightness. Can business be fun? Absolutely! It comes for different people in different ways, times, types, and tasks. It encompasses intuition, accomplishment and responsibility. It is *fundamental* to our nature; it is *funky* and whimsical; *functional*; and the *fund* from which all creativity springs. It is effortless.

It is our belief, proven in each corporate decision and experience thus far, that fun is the one pure and dependable measure of the integrity of our intention. If we have fun, we know we are on the right track. Each of us own total responsibility for our life's work. If fun isn't elemental in our relationships, endeavors, and communications, then we know we must swing from another vine.

Talk to us, we value your input. If you want to be on our mailing list— please send us your address.

THREE MONKEYS PUBLISHING
1535 CROOKS RD.
ROCHESTER HILLS, MI 48309
810•375-0688
http://www.threemonkeys.com

- OUR BOOKS MAKE GREAT GIFTS -
- ORDER FOR YOUR FRIENDS TODAY -
- IT'S EASY! -

Your order can be shipped to you, or directly to the person you wish to receive the gift. We'll even gift wrap it and enclose a card with a personal note from you, for a nominal cost, if requested. We will pay shipping/tax on all orders prepaid by check!

Corporate and volume discount programs available.

Just call us with your special requests.
(810) 375-0688

You can find out more about Three Monkeys Publishing and other books we publish on the Internet. Visit our Home Page at:

http://www.threemonkeys.com